What I'd like most of all is somebody to talk to. About my life. About how things are at home. See – I *know* why kids hate me. I know I seem weird to them, but it's not me. It's not. Inside I'm just like them. I like pop music and TV and clothes but I can't have them. They're forbidden. I'd like to have a party, invite everybody on my table, but I can't even bring a friend home. I mean, there are kids at church. Righteous kids. They see one another, play together, but not me. I can't bring anybody to the house in case they find out about Abomination. I can go to *their* homes – I used to – but I can never invite them back so they stopped bothering with me and you can't blame them, but if there was just one person who understood, one person who *knew*, I think I could stand it…

Martha

Other titles by Robert Swindells:

ROOM 13/INSIDE THE WORM OMNIBUS
NIGHTMARE STAIRS
ABOMINATION
A WISH FOR WINGS
BLITZED
RUBY TANYA
IN THE NICK OF TIME
TIMESNATCH

ROBERT SWINDELLS

Abomination

CORGI

ABOMINATION

A CORGI BOOK 9780552555883

First published in Great Britain by Doubleday,
an imprint of Random House Children's Publishers UK

Doubleday edition published 1998
Corgi Yearling edition published 1999
This edition 2007

16

Corgi Books are published by
Random House Children's Publishers UK
61–63 Uxbridge Road, London W5 5SA,
A Random House Group Company

Addresses for companies within The Random House Group Limited
can be found at: www.randomhouse.co.uk/offices.htm

THE RANDOM HOUSE GROUP Limited Reg. No. 954009
www.**randomhousechildrens**.co.uk

A CIP catalogue record for this book is available from the British Library.

Penguin Random House is committed to a sustainable future for
our business, our readers and our planet. This book is made from
Forest Stewardship Council® certified paper.

Printed and bound in Great Britain by Clays Ltd, St Ives plc

1. Martha

They chased me home again today and the new boy, Scott, joined in. When he smiled at me yesterday I hoped he was going to be my friend, but he's not. He was yelling Raggedy-Ann just like everybody else as I ran up Taylor Hill.

When I got in Mother said, 'You've been running.' I've never told her the kids chase me and she doesn't like me to run. I said, 'Yes, Mother, I'm sorry.' She shook her head like she does, tutting. 'There's a time, Martha,' she says. 'A time to every purpose under heaven.'

I hate my name. Martha. It's in the Bible but the kids think it's a stupid name. They call me Arthur or Ma, and that's when I'm lucky. Mostly it's

Raggedy-Ann, because of my clothes. Mother makes my clothes and I wish she didn't. They're good clothes and I know she sews them because she loves me, but they're different. I mean they're not rags or anything – that's not why they call me Raggedy-Ann. Mother would die before she let me wear rags, but they don't look right. You can see they're home-made. I mentioned it once, how all the kids have Nike trainers and jogging bottoms and stuff like that, but Mother just said, 'All is vanity.' There's a saying for everything in the Bible.

The kids don't know the Bible. Mother says they're raised in darkness like the heathen, but I don't know. I mean, I know the Bible's the word of God and God never lies, but it says the meek shall inherit the earth and I'm meek and the kids are not, and it seems to me they've inherited this little bit of the earth – the bit with me in it.

Anyway, today's Tuesday so it's lamb cutlets with green beans and mashed potatoes. Father says plain food's best. Good plain food, he calls it. We never have pizza or curry or fish and chips. We have cakes or biscuits sometimes, but they're home-made like my clothes. Father says shop ones are for idle people.

ABOMINATION

I never get to eat straight away, because one of my jobs is to feed Abomination. It's my worst thing. Worse than hair-pulling or name-calling or being chased. I hate the cellar, but that's where Abomination lives and so I have to go down there every single day. If the kids knew, maybe they'd leave me alone but they don't, because it's a secret. Nobody knows except Father and Mother and me. And God, I suppose. You can't keep secrets from God.

2. Scott

I think it's going to be all right, Southcott Middle. I'm in Mr Wheelwright's class. He's OK. Looks like Rolf Harris but likes computers and supports Man United so can't be all bad. The kids're OK too, apart from a snob or two and a few veg, but you always get those. There's a terrific playing-field, and at lunchtime after your meal you can play on the computers in the library. You've got to be quick, mind – there're only ten computers and it's first come first served, but that's fair. A great white shark can't wreck a dinner quicker than me.

Oh, I nearly forgot. There's this really weird girl, Martha Dewhurst. The kids laughed yesterday because Wheelwright put me on her table. I didn't know why they were laughing till morning break, when this guy called Simon came up to me and said, 'Keep your head away from Raggedy-Ann's if you don't want nits.' That's her nickname – Raggedy-Ann. I don't think she has nits, but there's like a gap between her and everybody else on our table, and nobody'll lend her their rubber. She has these funny clothes. I mean, they're *uniform* – maroon sweater, grey skirt – but they're not like everyone else's. I think her mum must've made them. Or her gran.

There's this game after school, Chase Raggedy-Ann. Some kid'll start chanting – *chase Raggedy-Ann, chase Raggedy-Ann* – like that. A few others join in, and when there's about ten they set off after her. I didn't go yesterday – felt a bit sorry for her if you must know – but I did today because Simon started it and he's my friend. She looks really funny, running. She's got these very thin, long legs that splay out sort of sideways as she runs, and her arms are all over the place too. I doubt she'll ever run for England. The kids don't try to catch her – it'd be over straight away if they did – so they hang back, running about fifty metres behind her, chanting *Raggedy-Ann,*

Raggedy-Ann, we'll all scrag you if we can. She doesn't seem to know they're not trying to catch her. You can tell she's going full belt. She lives up this very steep slope called Taylor Hill. Her house is near the top, and she's near collapsing by the time she reaches the gate. We pull up and watch her stagger up the path like a shot bandit, then we walk back down the hill, laughing and joking and taking turns with a ciggy.

I reckon I'll be fine at my new school.

3. Martha

My favourite time is after dinner when I have the place to myself. Father's an agent for an insurance company. He does his round at night because that's when people are in, and Mother works the evening shift at a soft toy factory.

I have the washing-up to do and Abomination's mess to see to, but after that I'm free till ten, except in winter when it's nine thirty. We don't have TV. I sometimes listen to Radio One, but I've got to remember not to leave the set tuned to that station when I switch off, because the Righteous believe the devil reaches young people through pop music. The Righteous is our church. One night last year I forgot, and when

Father switched on for the morning news he got Madonna and I got the rod. It's a cane really, but Father calls it the rod. His favourite text is *Train up a child in the way he should go: and when he is old, he will not depart from it*. Notice it says *he*, not *she*. It's not about girls, but Father seems not to have spotted that and I daren't point it out.

They're administered really carefully by the way, my beatings. Oh, yes. Wouldn't do for some busybody to spot the marks on me. They're always on my bum, so they're covered in PE and even when I swim. I could show somebody of course, but then Father would get into trouble and I wouldn't want to be responsible for that. He thinks he's doing the best thing, you see: that it's for my own good.

Anyway, after twirling round the kitchen to a few of the devil's tunes, I usually go up to my room and look at Mary's postcards. Mary's my big sister. Father sent her away when I was six. She's grown up and has a really interesting life if the cards are anything to go by. They're from all over: London, Liverpool, Birmingham. There's even one from Amsterdam. Some are addressed to Mother and Father and some are to me. I'm not supposed to have any of them. Father tears them up unread and throws them in the bin, but I rescue them and stick them back together with sellotape. I've been doing this since I was six. I couldn't read then, but I knew who they were from and the pictures were nice. I've got thirty-one now, in a shoe-box under the floor, with my Blur poster, four *Point Horror* books and a few other things my parents wouldn't like.

Mother says we're special because we're Righteous, but that doesn't make me feel better. I'd rather not be special if it means having to hide things.

If I can't have friends round.

If I can't have friends.

4. Scott

Saturday morning I'd arranged to meet Simon down town so he could show me round, but I nearly didn't get to keep the appointment. We lived near Birmingham before, and my folks never let me go into the city by myself. Twelve's too young they'd say, though some of my friends did it every weekend. When I mentioned it Friday night, there was a row. You'd no business making arrangements like that without asking, they said. We don't know this boy. This Simon. You better phone him and say you won't be there.

I talked 'em round, but only because I didn't have Simon's number. Dad said to look it up in the book, but I pretended I didn't know his surname. I do of course – it's Pritchard – but he wasn't to know that. In the end him and Mum decided that because Scratchley's a small place it would probably be OK. I was really chuffed – like they'd finally noticed I'm not a little kid any more. I felt like dancing round the room, thumping the air and going *Yes!*, but I didn't. I acted dead cool.

Lying in bed that night I started thinking about Martha. Don't ask me why. I'd helped chase her home Wednesday and Thursday, but I hadn't joined in today and neither had Simon. We'd been too busy making our arrangements. Others had gone after her though. I don't think she ever gets to just walk home like everybody else. I feel sorry for her in a way but she makes me angry too. I know that sounds strange, but it's a fact. It irritates me the way she puts up with everything. I mean, if she told someone – Mr Wheelwright or one of the other teachers – they'd *do* something, wouldn't they? They'd put a stop to it, or try to. At the very least there'd be an Assembly about bullying. And in class, she pretends not to notice the space round her chair, or that nobody speaks to her. She doesn't ask to borrow anything or try to start a conversation. She sits with her eyes down, concentrating on her work, and if Wheelwright asks her a question she ignores the sniggers and answers quietly, and it's usually the right answer. It's as if nothing can push her over the edge. She's like some helpless little animal. Never cries.

Anyway I lay a long time thinking about her and had a restless night, so that when I met Simon in the shopping centre it felt more like ten at night than ten in the morning. I wondered what he'd say if I told him I was being bugged by Raggedy-Ann. Not that I would. When you've only one friend, you want to keep him.

5. Martha

Scott lent me his ruler today. I'd used mine at home and forgotten to put it back in my bag. I didn't ask him. He saw me rummaging and said, 'Lost something?' 'Yes,' I whispered. 'My ruler.' I expected him to snigger and say tough or something like that, but he didn't. He just pushed his ruler towards me. I looked up to see if he meant to snatch it away when I went to pick it up, but he was writing. I underlined my heading and slid the ruler back across the table. 'Thanks.' ''S'OK.' He didn't look up. Tracy Stamper snorted. 'I'd burn that now if I were you. It's contaminated.' Scott ignored her.

I know what you're thinking. You're thinking,

So what? Why's she banging on about someone lending her their ruler? Well, I know it's no big deal to you. Kids borrow one another's stuff all the time, but not me. Nobody ever lent me anything till today, or borrowed anything of mine. So although it only happened that one time, and though Scott didn't speak or even look at me again, it mattered. It made my day. I didn't even mind when they chased me home. In fact I was glad, because Scott wasn't with them. If you've never been ignored it'll just sound daft to you.

What I'd like most of all is somebody to talk to. About my life. About how things are at home. See – I *know* why the kids hate me. I know I seem weird to them, but it's not me. It's not. Inside I'm just like them. I like pop music and TV and clothes but I can't have them. They're forbidden. I'd like to have a party, invite everybody on my table, but I can't even bring a friend home. I mean, there are kids at church. Righteous kids. They see one another, play together, but not me. I can't bring anybody to the house in case they find out about Abomination. I can go to *their* homes – I used to – but I never invited them back so they stopped bothering with me and you can't blame them, but if there was just one person who understood, one person who *knew*, I think I could stand it.

So. It's seven o'clock, my parents are out and I'm lying on my bed constructing a fantasy. I do this a lot. It's my way of escaping for a while. This particular fantasy is different from most because it's based on fact – the fact that Scott lent me his ruler. In my fantasy, I go up to him at break and thank him, and we get talking and it turns out he fancies me. Wants to take me out. We go to a live Blur concert. My parents think I'm at Bible class. From then on we're inseparable, Scott and me. One day he finds Gordon Linfoot giving me an Indian burn behind the bike sheds and beats him up. Another time it's a maths exam and he's completely stuck and I slip him all the answers on a bit of paper. We come joint top, and to celebrate we take a train to London, staying in a posh hotel and buying all the latest fashions on Oxford Street. Mother and Father know nothing about it – they're in comas after a car crash.

Amazing what it can lead to, borrowing someone's ruler.

6. Scott

It was good in town. Simon got there about a minute after me, and we checked out this games shop and a few other places in the Centre before he showed me the town. There's not a lot in Scratchley. All the good shops are in the Centre. The best bit apart from that is the park. A river runs through town and the park's on both banks, with a footbridge connecting the two halves. It's got a bike track, a place for skateboards and a café with tables inside and outside where they do burgers and Coke and stuff. Kids go there Saturdays. We saw Tracy Stamper and another girl from school. Tracy said to me, 'If you're waiting for Raggedy-Ann, you're wasting your time. She never comes here.' What a spack. I suppose she said it because I lent Martha my ruler. 'I'm not waiting for anybody,' I told her, 'and if I was it wouldn't be you.'

The other cool place is the library, because on the top floor there's a room where they some-times shoot *Nickelodeon*. There's a sign on the steps – *GROWN-UP-FREE ZONE* – and the room's all done out with like posters and mobiles and giant fluffy toys. I was buzzing, but there was nobody around. Simon's had free pencils and puzzles and lots of other stuff from there, and once they videoed him and he saw himself on telly. 'We'll check it out next week,' he said.

When we got hungry, we went back to the park and ate. It was warm and sunny so we sat outside. Tracy and her friend had gone. We ordered Cheesy Bigburgers with fries and drank Cokes while we waited, and it was not what you'd call fast food. You could have eaten at McDonald's and been halfway to Australia by the time it came, but it was good.

'Have you been told about the Expedition?' asked Simon between bites. I shook my head.

'Oh, it's great. Year Eight goes every summer,

after half-term. Three days. Place called Hang-lands. Canoeing, caving, abseiling, you name it. It's seventy pounds. See Killer Kilroy about it.' Mr Kilroy was PE and boys' games.

'Does everybody go?'

'Not everybody. Some parents don't want their kid abseiling and stuff. They think it's dangerous. And some can't afford it.'

'So what do the kids do for three days – those who stay behind I mean?'

Simon shrugged. 'They help kids in other years, or Chocky finds 'em jobs to do.' Chocky's the Head, Mr Cadbury. Simon grinned. 'I bet I know someone who won't be going.'

'Who?' I knew, but I wanted to prove she wasn't on my mind.

'I'll give you a clue. She's on your table.'

'Martha?'

'Correct. Have a House Point.'

She *was* on my mind though. Had been all morning. *What does Martha do Saturdays? Does she have fun? Does she know what fun is? And why the heck do I care?* I didn't *want* to think about the sad spack, for Pete's sake. In fact it was doing my head in, but I couldn't help it. I kept seeing that pasty face, the hair that looked like it had been styled with a knife and fork, those big, awful eyes.

Hey: maybe she's a witch. Maybe she cast a spell on me by touching my ruler.

7. Martha

What do you do, Sundays? Sleep late, eat a big breakfast, go for a run in the car? Most people seem to, ending up at garden centres, Sunday markets, tourist spots. A few pop into church first, but not many. Nice day anyway – something to look forward to all week.

Let me tell you about *my* Sunday. My Sabbath. The Sabbath of the Righteous.

It kicks off at six, summer and winter. Rain or shine.

My alarm goes off. I get up, wash my hands and face in cold water, put on the brown dress Mother sewed for me, make my bed and tidy my room. If it is winter, I do all of this in the dark. At six forty-five, I go downstairs. There's no electric light, no heat, no breakfast. Just a candle burning at Father's end of the table, where he sits with the big Bible. At the other end, in darkness if it is winter, sits Mother. *Good morning, Martha*, says Father. *Good morning, Father*, I reply. *Good morning, Martha*, says Mother. *Good morning, Mother*, say I, and sit down. The floor is of quarry tiles, and I take care not to make a screeching sound with the legs of my chair. The Bible is open at the page Father wants. After leading the two of us in a short prayer, he reads a story from the Old Testament. It might be the story of Esau and Jacob, or Gideon, or Samson, or Jonah, or some other story. I know them all. When he's finished he says, *The word of God*, and closes the Bible. By this time it's about seven fifteen. We can hear Abomination making noises in the cellar because there's been no food, but nobody mentions this.

We get ready for church. It's a mile away and we walk. We've missed only once since I was born. It had snowed all night and there'd been a high wind. Some of the drifts were five feet deep. I was six years old. We set off, but had to turn back. Father had sent Mary away just a few days before. He said the blocked road was God punishing him for raising such a daughter. I remember thinking it might be God punishing him for turning her out of the house, but of course I didn't say anything. Perhaps I didn't think it – not at six. Maybe it occurred to me when I was a bit older. Anyway.

Meeting starts at eight fifteen and usually goes on till eleven. Yes, that's right – two and three quarter hours solid of praying and listening. The building is cold and bare. The seats are hard wooden chairs and we mustn't fidget. Even the youngest kids have to sit absolutely still and pay attention. You want to try it sometime, in midwinter when you're hungry and your feet are wet because the snow came over your boots. Tell yourself God loves you. It won't help.

The walk home warms us, and when we get in we're permitted to return to the twentieth century. Father switches on the central heating and Mother microwaves a stew she made yesterday. I'm sent down the cellar to feed Abomination, which is horrible, but then comes the highlight of my day – I get to eat.

In the afternoon I do my homework while Father studies the Bible and Mothers sews. At five we walk to six o'clock Meeting. Those chairs again, this time for about an hour. Then the walk home (normal people whizzing past us in cars at the end of their day out), a mug of cocoa, then bed.

There's this text in a frame on the dining-room wall. *Six days shall work be done: but the seventh day is the sabbath of rest.*

That's what it says, so why is it that when Sunday night rolls round I'm more shattered than I've been all week?

8. Scott

I spotted Martha Sunday afternoon. It was just after five. We'd been to Borley Water Gardens, and as we drove up Wentworth Road there she was, walking down with two wrinklies. Her parents, probably. You should have seen them. The sun was shining and it was still warm, but the guy was wearing a thick black overcoat that came nearly to his ankles and a black, wide-brimmed hat, and the woman was in a shapeless brown thing they'd be ashamed to hang in a charity shop. She wore a beat-up old hat that looked like a rat had crawled on to her head and died. Martha was in brown too, walking between her folks with her head down. If my parents looked like that, I'd walk with my head down. I waved as we zoomed past, but I know she didn't see me because I asked her, Monday morning.

Well, I felt sorry for her. Plus I wanted to know where she'd been off to at five o'clock Sunday afternoon. It was just before the nine o'clock buzzer. She was standing by herself as usual, near the staffroom window. I drifted over there, trying to make it look accidental. I'd nothing against her myself but I didn't want it to look like I was seeking her company.

'Hi.'

'Oh . . . hello, Scott.' She blushed. First time I'd seen her in colour.

'Didn't see me yesterday, did you?'

'Yesterday? Where?'

'Wentworth Road. Teatime. You were walking down. We drove past.'

'Oh.' She shook her head. 'No, I didn't see you.'

'I waved.'

'Did you? Thanks, but I'm afraid I didn't notice.'

'You don't have to thank me; it was just a wave. Were those your folks?'

'Yes. Mother and Father. We were on our way to church.'

'Ah-ha. Which church is that, then?'

'You won't know it. It's the Church of the Righteous on Hustler Street, but it doesn't look like a church. No spire or anything.'

'Right. What happens there – anything good?'

'I . . . don't know what you mean. It's a church. You know what happens at church.'

'No, I don't. I've never been. I suppose it's kind of like a school assembly, isn't it?'

'Well, it's a bit more . . . serious than that. And longer.'

'But you see friends there?'

She shrugged. 'Sort of. They don't bother with me much because I'm not allowed to invite anybody home.'

'Why's that?'

'Because . . . my father says so.'

'Do you always do what your father tells you?'

'Well, yes – don't *you*?'

'Not always. Have you brothers, Martha? Or sisters?'

'No, there's only me.' She frowned. 'Why are you asking me all these questions, Scott?'

'Oh, I was wondering, that's all. I'll see you later, OK?'

I'd stood with her longer than I'd meant to. I moved on and she called after me, 'Yes, Scott. Later.' I didn't look back.

9. Martha

'You're looking happy, Martha. Have you had a good day at school?'

'Yes, Father.' It's half past six. We're eating dinner. It's liver but for once I don't mind.

'Did you win a House Point?' asks Mother.

'No.'

'Then what?'

'The new boy. Scott. He talked to me. Asked me things.'

'What sort of things, Martha?' Father's tone is sharp.

'Oh – things about me. He saw us yesterday in Wentworth Road and waved. I didn't see him.'

'What did he ask you, child?'

'I don't remember exactly. If you were my folks. Where we were going. If I had sisters or brothers.'

'And how did you answer that?'

'I said there was only me.'

'Good. Now listen to me, Martha.' He sets down his knife and fork. He's about to spoil it all. I know he is. 'To have a friend is a pleasant thing. Mother and I want you to have lots of friends, but you must understand that we of the Righteous are different from other people – so different that they often find us strange. If you let yourself become too fond of this boy, you will be badly hurt when he finds he can't relate to your way of life and drops you.'

A lump comes to my throat. Does my father think I'm not badly hurt already? Can't he see I just want to be like everybody else? I shake my head. 'I'm not fond of him, Father. He talked to me, that's all. Please say I can be his friend if he'll let me.'

He sighs, shaking his head. 'I'm only trying to shield you from unhappiness, child. Be this boy's friend if it pleases you, but be careful. Guard your tongue at all times, and don't bring him home.'

Don't bring him home. They don't know how I hate my home: that if I had my way I wouldn't bring *myself* home, never mind anyone else.

10. Scott

I blew it with Simon, Tuesday morning. Lost my
first friend at Southcott Middle, and all because
of Martha.

It was such a *little* thing, that's what gets me.
Old Wheelwright asked a question and Martha
put her hand up and when he said, 'Yes,
Martha?', Simon kicked her under the table so she
went 'Ow!' 'What on *earth's* the matter?' goes
Wheelwright, and instead of splitting on Simon,
Martha says, 'Nothing sir,' and Wheelwright
says, 'It didn't *sound* like nothing, Martha,' and
lets somebody else answer. All I did was glare at
Simon and growl, 'Don't you ever get fed-up,
picking on the same person all the time?' I don't

even know why I said it. Anyway, it didn't go down too well. 'Funny you should say that,' purrs Simon, 'because it *is* getting a bit boring. I reckon it's time we had a fresh target, and you just volunteered.'

I thought nothing of it at the time. Took it as a joke, but when break rolled round he wouldn't talk to me. 'Shove off, Coxon,' he snarled, and walked away.

Something worse happened at lunchtime. I was walking down the hall with my tray when Gordon Linfoot stuck his foot out. I sort of dived forward and my tray went up in the air. Everybody cheered as the two plates shattered on the floor, flinging gravy and custard far and wide. Chocky jumped up from the teachers' table and came hurrying towards me as I staggered to my feet.

'What the blazes were you playing at, boy?'

'Sir . . .' I nodded towards Linfoot. 'He tripped me up, sir.'

'I didn't, sir – look!' Gordon pointed to my shoe. 'His lace is undone.'

It was. Just my luck. Chocky made me fetch a mop and bucket and stood over me while I picked everything up and swabbed the parquet with practically the whole school watching. I was blushing so much it felt like my cheeks were on fire. When I'd finished, Chocky sent me to stand outside his door till afternoon lessons began. No dinner, and no chance to pulverize Linfoot in the yard, which is what I felt like doing. *Never mind*, I thought, *it'll wait till hometime*. I'd no way of knowing things were about to get far worse.

11. Scott

Half three. Linfoot must've known I'd be after him, because by the time I got to the cloakroom he'd gone. I grabbed my jacket and ran outside and there they were in a half-circle round the door, waiting for me. Simon, Tracy, two lads called Gerry Latimer and Paul Mawson who always chase Martha, and Gordon himself. I pulled up and stood looking at them, wondering what they meant to do.

Simon smiled. 'Looking for someone, were you, Coxon?'

'Yes, him.' I nodded towards Linfoot.

'Gordon? Why – what's he done?'

'He knows.'

Simon looked at Linfoot. 'What you done to Coxon, Gor?'

Linfoot shrugged. 'Nothing, Simon. Not that I know of.'

Simon turned to me. 'Says he didn't do anything to you, Coxon.'

'He's a liar.'

'Hear that, Gor? Coxon here reckons you're a liar.'

'Naw. It's *him* who's the liar, Simon. Telling Chocky I tripped him.'

'Oooh!' Simon shook his head. 'Lied to *Chocky*, did he? That's serious. That reflects on the whole class, as Wheely might say. I don't know about you guys, but I reckon he deserves to be punished for that.'

'Yeah,' nodded Gordon, 'I think you're right.'

'Absolutely,' murmured Tracy. The others indicated agreement. Simon gazed at me, smiling and frowning at the same time. 'Question is, how?'

'I know.' This from Tracy.

Simon looked at her. 'What d'you suggest, Tracy?'

'I suggest he deserves his own song, same as Raggedy-Ann.'

'Hmm – got anything in mind, have you?'

'I might have.'

'Go on then.'

'Well, how about, *Snotty Scotty, Snotty Scotty, brain is dead and clothes are grotty*?'

A chorus of enthusiastic noises greeted Tracy's suggestion, and it was then I realized the whole thing must've been thought up and rehearsed at lunchtime. I mean, it wasn't a brilliant song, but it was too good for Tracy Stamper to have made up right there and then. Anyway, before I knew what was happening Simon darted forward and pulled me into the middle of them and they were dancing round me, kicking and punching and singing the song. I swung my bag, trying to break out of the ring, but somebody grabbed it and jerked and I went sprawling and shoe leather started coming from all directions, thudding into me. I thought, *this is it, they're gonna kick me to death*, but then I heard a shout and the kids scattered and next thing I knew Killer Kilroy was squatting next to me and Martha looking over his shoulder. Turned out she saw them laying into me and ran to get a teacher. Didn't boost her popularity I can tell you. Or mine.

12. Martha

I only saw because I'd decided to hang back. I thought, I'll wait till everybody's gone, then walk home for once instead of running, so I locked myself in the toilet and waited. After ten minutes it was dead quiet so I came out. I was tiptoeing across the porch, listening, when some kids started chanting. I could hear thuds and cries as well, and I knew somebody was getting beaten up.

I nearly went back to the toilets. I don't know why I didn't. Something stopped me, that's all I know. I crept to the doorway and peeped out and it was Scott, surrounded by all these kids. As I watched, he fell down and they started kicking him, and I knew it was my fault. He'd spoken up for me when Simon Pritchard kicked me in class, so they'd turned on him.

I didn't know what to do. If I was brave, I'd have charged at them, punching and kicking to rescue my friend, but I'm not so I turned and ran back, heading for the staffroom. As I crossed the hall, Mr Kilroy came out of the PE store and yelled, '*Walk*, girl, don't run!'

'Please sir,' I gasped, 'there's a gang beating a kid up in the yard.'

I don't like Mr Kilroy because he's sarky to kids who're useless at PE but give him his due – he didn't hang about. 'Show me,' he rapped, so I ran and he followed. When the kids saw him coming they ran like rabbits. Scott was lying on the ground. Mr Kilroy knelt beside him and talked to him and sort of examined him and I wouldn't have believed it, he was so gentle. All I could do was stand like a lemon, watching. When he'd made sure nothing was broken he helped Scott to his feet and steered him inside. I trailed after. They went in the First-Aid room where Killer used cotton wool and antiseptic to clean the cuts and grazes on Scott's face and hands. I stood in the doorway. Scott knew I was there but he wouldn't look at me. I wondered if I should leave. I was about to when Mr Kilroy turned.

'Do you two live in the same direction?'

'Yes,' I said, though we don't. Scott frowned but didn't contradict me.

'Good,' smiled Killer, 'then you can walk the patient home, Martha. It *is* Martha, isn't it?'

I nodded. If you're no good at games, Killer doesn't know you.

'Splendid. Off you go then. Oh . . .' He looked at Scott. 'I shall want the names of your attackers, lad. First thing in the morning, OK?'

'Yessir.'

'Where d'you live?' I asked, when we'd walked side by side across the yard without speaking.

'Dinsdale Rise,' he murmured. 'Why did you tell Killer we lived in the same direction?'

'Because . . . I knew he hoped we did. And because it's my fault they set on you.'

'*Your* fault? How d'you make that out?'

'Well – they did it because of what you said to Simon, didn't they?'

'Maybe, but I chose to say it so you're not to blame.'

'I *feel* responsible.'

'Well, you're not.' He stopped. 'Look, you don't have to walk me home, Martha. I'm fine, honestly. It's miles out of your way.'

'I don't mind. I *want* to walk you home.'

'Won't your folks wonder why you're late?'

'No.' They would, but I didn't care. Not at that moment.

'Well . . . if you're sure.' He gave me a shy smile. 'Thanks for rescuing me, by the way.'

I shook my head. 'Killer rescued you. I wish it *had* been me.' I shouldn't have said that. I know I shouldn't. It just slipped out.

He laughed. 'Why d'you wish that?'

'Well, because . . . I like you, I suppose.'

He nodded. 'I like you, too.' His expression grew serious. 'You know they'll give us a hard time tomorrow, don't you? You for bringing Killer, me because they hadn't finished kicking me.'

I shrugged. 'They give me a hard time *every* day, Scott. I'm used to it.' I grinned briefly. 'I know it's a funny thing to say, but it'll be nice not to be the only one.'

He chuckled. 'I know what you mean. Anyway here we are – Dinsdale Rise. I live at number eight. Fancy coming in for a Coke or something?'

I fancied it all right. I'd have loved to have seen the inside of his home, but I shook my head. 'Better not. Mother'll be worried. Thanks anyway.'

He pulled a face. 'No prob. See you tomorrow. Oh – and thanks for walking me.'

'I enjoyed it.'

I watched till he closed the door, then set off back. I knew there'd be trouble when I got home, but I was glad I'd walked with Scott.

13. Unlucky for Some

'What on earth's happened to your face, Scott love?' She's a worrier, my mum.

'It's nothing, Mum. We were having a game. Got a bit carried away, I guess.'

'You certainly did. And who's the girl?'

'Girl?'

'The one you were with just now.'

'Oh.' That's another thing about my mum. Eyes like a hawk. 'Just someone from school. We walked on together.'

'Ah – so *that's* why you're late, is it?' She twinkled. 'Bit of courting, eh?'

'No.' I shook my head. 'No way. I don't even like her.'

'Didn't look as though you were saying goodbye to someone you *hate*, Scott. What's her name?'

'Martha.'

'What an old-fashioned name. Haven't come across a Martha for years.'

I nodded. 'She's an old-fashioned girl.'

'Nice name, though. I like it. You should've invited her in, Scott.'

'I did, but she wouldn't.'

Mum chuckled. 'I thought you said you didn't like her.'

'Yeah, well . . .' I left the kitchen to hang up my jacket so she wouldn't see me blushing. Why do parents have to bang on about *courting* every time they happen to see you within fifty metres of a girl? It's embarrassing.

*

'What time do you call *this*, Martha?' There they sit, the pair of them, gazing at me across the table. They've waited dinner for me. Animal noises from below tell me Abomination's had to wait too. I look at my watch. 'It's ten to five, Father.'

He nods. 'Ten to five. Your mother had dinner ready at four-fifteen as usual. We've been sitting here for thirty-five minutes listening to that racket

47

from the cellar, and now the food is spoiled. What have you to say to us?'

'I'm sorry, Father. Sorry, Mother. Somebody needed my help. At school. I had to give it.'

'Who, Martha? Who needed this help?'

'Scott. The boy I told you about.'

'Ah. I see. And this help – what form did it take?'

'He was being beaten. By a gang. I ran for a teacher.'

'And this took thirty-five minutes?'

'No. The teacher – Mr Kilroy – gave first aid. I watched.'

'Why?'

'Because . . . it was my fault Scott got hurt. He stuck up for me.'

'I see. And *after* the first aid?'

'The teacher asked me to walk Scott home.'

'The teacher *asked* you? Why, Martha.'

'I suppose he thought Scott might have delayed concussion or something, Father.'

'And *did* he?'

'No, Father.'

'No.' Father shakes his head. 'Scott did *not* have delayed concussion, but your family had delayed dinner.'

'I'm sorry, Father.'

'So you have said, and I mean to make you a great deal sorrier presently. You will see to Abomination's dinner, then go to your room. I will be up to correct you when your mother and I have broken bread.'

Up to correct you. I don't need to tell you what *that* means, do I? I wish somebody'd tell *me* something though: what's the difference between what the Good Samaritan did for the man who fell among thieves, and what I did for Scott?

14. Martha

When Father left my room, locking the door to keep me from reaching food in the night, I got my postcards out. It helps to look at them when I've been corrected, because they're from other places. Places Father's never seen and never will. Places I'll go as soon as I'm old enough, like Mary. She was here, under his thumb, and it must've seemed to her it would never end but it did. The rod didn't keep her here. It drove her away, that and the cold Sunday mornings and the good plain food.

Birmingham's my favourite. It shows a sort of fountain with a stone lady lying in it, but it's not the picture I like. It's what Mary wrote on the back. She was writing to me and I was only seven so she didn't do joined-up writing. That's how I know she's nice. It says:

Dearest Marfa (her pet name for me – I couldn't pronounce *th* when I was learning to talk)

I hope you're OK, as I am. Birmingham is big and full of interesting things, like this fountain. I have found a friend. She's called Annette. I wish you could meet her, she's so funny. You won't forget your big sister will you, poppet? She loves and misses you every day. I'll write again soon. Be a good girl.

Mary

You won't forget your big sister. Always makes me cry, that bit. As if I would. *Jezebel*, Father calls her, when he mentions her at all, but she's got something he'll never have. She's got my love.

I hope it reaches her. My love, I mean. I send it to her when I'm in bed. I don't know where she is because she never puts her address, so I send it

51

through the air like a radio station. I picture it, spreading through the darkness like the ripples when a pebble plops into a pond. It goes in every direction so some of it's bound to find her, isn't it?

15. Scott

I do like Martha, though. I've no idea why. She's definitely weird – the kids are right about that but what I think is, just because someone's weird isn't a good reason to pick on them. I mean, you get to know a weird person – really *know* them – and I bet you'll find there's a reason why they're the way they are, and it won't be their fault.

I was thinking about all this stuff in bed Tuesday night, because I couldn't sleep. I kept wondering what Martha's folks said to her when she got home. Did she get in trouble? They'd looked seriously strange walking down Wentworth Road, and that's what I mean – maybe Martha just takes after them.

I was right about Wednesday morning. They did give us a hard time. Me, anyway. I walked through the gateway and the same bunch was waiting. They went straight into the chant. I'd expected something of the sort and walked on, not looking at them. They followed me across the yard going, *Snotty Scotty, snotty Scotty, brain is dead and clothes are grotty*. Other kids joined in. When I still ignored them, Simon and Gordon started pushing me in the back. They were trying to make me fight, but I'm not daft. You can't fight five people. I escaped by going inside. You can go in to use the toilet, but if a bunch go in together the teachers chuck 'em out.

I hung about the cloakroom till the buzzer went. Martha kept looking at me as old Wheelwright marked the register. I'd a couple of plasters on my face. I caught her eye and she gave me a sympathetic smile.

Straight after registration, a kid came in and told Wheely that Killer wanted to see me. He didn't *say* Killer, of course. Wheely nodded. 'Yes, all right. Off you go, Scott.' He was eyeing the plasters too.

Killer was setting out apparatus in the gym. He looked me up and down.

'Now, young Scott – how're you this morning?'

'I'm fine, sir, thanks.'

'That's the way, laddie. Now.' He produced a notebook and pencil. 'Who were they?'

'I dunno, sir.'

He glanced up sharply. 'You don't know? A bunch of your classmates uses you as a football and you don't know who they are?'

'I'm new, sir. I don't know everybody's name yet.'

'Uh-huh. You could point 'em out to me though?'

'I don't think so, sir.'

'You don't think so?'

'No, sir.'

'I see, or at least I think I do.' He sighed. 'You don't have to put up with it, y'know.'

'Sir?'

'Bullying, lad. You don't have to put up with it. Oh, I know – they threaten awful things if you split on 'em, but they're kids, Scott, not the Mafia. We can sort 'em out quick-sticks once we know who they are, but we need names. You'll be sure and come to me if you – er – *remember* any names, won't you?'

'Yessir.'

'Yessir.' He sighed again. 'All right, Scott – off you pop.'

He returned to his apparatus and I went back to my class, wondering why I'd acted as I had. A couple of days ago I was mad at Martha for taking it and not splitting, and here I was doing the same thing myself.

I swear she's put a spell on me with her sad grey eyes. They haunt me, those eyes.

16. Martha

When Scott came back from seeing Killer, Simon muttered, 'Grass us up did you, Snotty?' and Scott said, 'No.'

Simon smirked. 'You're not as daft as you look.'

'I will, though,' said Scott, 'if you don't lay off Martha.'

'Oooh!' went Tracy. 'Sticking up for the girl-friend, eh? You wouldn't be so fond if you had to sit next to her, like me.'

Scott looked at her. 'D'you want to swap places?'

Tracy sniggered. 'Beam me up, Snotty.'

So they changed places. It was nice to have

someone next to me who didn't move his chair as far away as possible. It still happened at lunchtime though, because he has a meal and I bring sandwiches and we use different parts of the hall. There's always empty chairs near me.

A good thing happened at hometime, but it was spoiled later by a bad thing. I was loitering near the cloakroom, waiting till everybody had gone, when Scott came up to me.

'Come on,' he grinned, 'my turn to walk you home.'

I didn't know what to say. I mean, I was glad I wouldn't be leaving the building by myself, but I daren't let him walk me home. Suppose Father looked out the window? Or Mother? Suppose we were seen by someone from church? He sensed my hesitation and slipped his hand under my elbow, steering me out the door.

We both expected the usual gang to be waiting, but when we got outside Killer was by the gate. He wasn't doing anything, just standing with his hands in his pockets but the yard was practically empty. Scott let go my arm pretty fast when he saw the teacher.

'G'night, Martha,' murmured Killer as we walked past. 'G'night, Scott.'

'G'night, sir,' we replied.

He didn't take my arm again, and we didn't talk. I wanted to, but I couldn't think of anything to say. I suppose it was the same for him. We kept sneaking looks at each other and when our eyes met we'd smile and look away. His cheeks looked hot and mine definitely were. When we reached the bottom of the hill, I stopped and said, 'You'd better not come any further, Scott.'

'Why not? I might as well walk you to the top.'

'No. My parents might see you.'

He shrugged. 'So what if they do? We're not doing anything.'

'They know you don't go home this way. They'd wonder why you came out of your way.'

'Tell 'em I'm your bodyguard.' He started uphill.

'No, Scott, please.' He turned with a frown and I said, 'It's our church, you see. The Righteous. It makes us different. I can't explain.'

He made an impatient sound. 'I thought we were friends, Martha. I want to see you home. Why is that such a problem?'

I shook my head. 'It isn't, Scott. Not for you. Not for most people, but my parents . . .'

'OK.' He lifted his hands, palms towards me.

'I get the message. I'm off.' He looked at me. 'I'm the new kid at school, Martha. I wanted to fit in, you know, without hassle? Now everybody calls me Snotty Scotty and I get roughed up because I took your part, and you won't even let me near your gate. D'you think that's fair?'

'I . . .'

'Doesn't matter. See you tomorrow.'

He walked off. I gazed after him for a while but he didn't look back.

17. Scott

I felt seriously depressed walking home. It's hard enough moving to a new district, starting at a strange school and befriending its least popular pupil, but when she turns round and practically tells you to get lost, well, it's a bummer to say the least. And of course the minute I walk in the door, Mum goes, 'Your turn to walk *her* home today, I suppose?' Parents.

Martha was all over me next morning, but I acted cool. I sat next to her and everything, but I grunted in response to her desperate chat. I wanted her to see I was mad, and I think she got the message. Others certainly did. First period Tracy whispers, 'Off her already, eh, Snotty?

Want your old seat back?' I shook my head.

Sensing her misery, they got up a mob at morning break to chase her. 'Join in, Snotty,' says Linfoot. I didn't, but I didn't stick up for her either. I lounged in a corner pretending to watch a pogs game while she gangled across the playing-field like a giraffe with three legs. *Raggedy-Ann, Raggedy-Ann, we'll all scrag you if we can.* I felt bad, but a guy who's good enough to stick up for you is good enough to walk you to your gate.

I didn't keep it up though. I couldn't. I saw her at lunchtime, across the hall, sitting in the middle of all these empty chairs while the other sand-wich-munchers scrunched together, chatting and laughing. Wonder what's in her sandwiches, I thought. Treacle? Cold porridge? Spiders? From the look on her face it had to be spiders.

I found her ten minutes later, standing on the pathway outside the staffroom window. If you stand there people tend to leave you alone, but it's a rotten way to spend your break because everyone knows why you're there, including the teachers. I went up to her.

'How's it going?'

She shrugged, scraping an invisible pattern on

the concrete flag with the toe of her shoe. 'You know – the usual.'

'Ah-ha. What d'you get in your sandwiches?'

'What?'

'Your sandwiches. What's in 'em, usually?'

'Oh. Spam. Cheese spread. Depends.'

'Not spiders, then?'

'*Spiders*?'

'Yeah, things could be worse, see?' I smiled. 'It could be spiders.'

'You're crazy.'

'I know. Teachers drive me crazy, spying on me. Let's move.'

She followed me on to the field. I saw Linfoot notice us together and run to tell Simon. Martha murmured, 'Scott?'

'Yeah?' We stood by the goal-posts. Gerry Latimer was in goal.

'I'm sorry about yesterday. I wanted to explain, but you see, Father doesn't like me talking to people about our affairs.'

I shrugged. 'It's OK, Martha. I'm not nosy. I just wondered why you didn't want your folks to see me. I mean, I don't have two heads or anything and I don't eat girls. In fact I'm harmless.'

She nodded. 'I know. It's just . . . well, I'm scared of my father, Scott. He beats me.'

'He *beats* you?' I stared at her. 'That's against the law, Martha. People can't *do* that any more.'

'He's my father.'

'Doesn't mean he can hit you. You should *tell* someone, stupid.'

'Who?'

'Oh, I dunno – the police, I suppose.'

'I couldn't do that. You can't set the police on your own *father*, for goodness sake.'

'Sure you can. *I* would.'

She shook her head. 'No you wouldn't, Scott. Not if it came to it.'

'Yes I would. If he beat me I would. No danger.'

'Well, you wouldn't if you belonged to the Righteous, Scott. We have our own ways, see.'

'You don't have your own *laws*, Martha. Everybody has to obey the law.'

She sighed. 'I knew you wouldn't understand. Nobody does. That's why it's no use trying to explain. That's why I don't go to the teachers about Simon Pritchard and the others. They'd say what you just said.'

'But you can't . . . go on taking it, Martha. I'll help you. We'll find a way out, you'll see.'

'No.' She smiled sadly. 'There's only one way out, Scott, and that's Mary's way.'

'Who the heck's Mary?'

'Mary's my . . .' She broke off as the buzzer went. We walked towards school. 'If you really want to know about Mary, I'll tell you at home-time.'

I nodded. 'I'll be by the gate.'

If I'm not on the ground being kicked to death, I thought.

18. Martha

Killer was by the gate again so there was no hassle. He probably thinks we're an item, Scott and me. When we were well past him, Scott said, 'Your turn to walk me, I think.'

'I *can't* Scott, you know that. If I'm late again, my father . . .'

'I know, Martha. Just kidding. Who's Mary, then?'

'My sister. Grown-up sister.'

'You said there was only you.'

'Well, there is, she doesn't live with us now.'

'Where *does* she live?'

'I don't know. She writes, but doesn't put her address.'

'Why not, for Pete's sake?'

'I think it's because she doesn't want my parents to know where she is.'

Scott chuckled. 'I don't blame her. Did they beat her too?'

'Oh, yes. She was braver than me. She used to stay out, see boys. I don't remember much about it really. Father sent her away when I was six.'

'And that's what you meant by Mary's way – getting out?'

'Yes.'

'So why don't you do it?'

'Because I'm only twelve, Scott. Where would I go? How would I eat?'

Scott shrugged. 'Isn't there a granny or an auntie or someone who'd take you in, if you told 'em what was going on?'

'No, Scott, there isn't. I mean, I've got two grannies and three aunties, but they're all in our church. They know what's *going on*, as you put it, and think it's perfectly normal.'

'So you're stuck with it till you're about sixteen?'

'Yes.'

'Glad I'm not you.' He looked at me. 'Can you . . . do they let you out Saturdays?'

'Sometimes. Depends what there is to do at home. Mother sends me to Asda – the super-market – most Saturdays.'

'You don't go in the car?'

'No. Father's an insurance man. He's out on his round, Saturdays.'

'So you have to lug everything home?'

I nodded. 'It's not bad, Scott. We don't shop like other people. There's only two bags most weeks.'

'Can I meet you?' He grinned. 'I could carry one of the bags. Part of the way at least.'

I shook my head. 'I don't know, Scott. I mean, it'd be great, but if somebody saw us . . .'

'Martha.' He reached out and took hold of both my hands. I felt like somebody in a film. 'Listen. You can't leave like your sister, but you could do some of the things she did. Stay out. See boys.' He smiled. 'This boy, anyway. It's *your* life.'

I shook my head again. 'I told you – Mary was brave; I'm not. They'd lock me up. Starve me. It's best to do what they want till I'm old enough to leave.'

'No it's not. Anyway, tell you what I'll do. I'll hang around Asda, Saturday morning. If I see you, we'll take it from there. How's that?'

I looked at him. 'You're crazy. You could wait hours.'

'I will, if I have to.'

'D'you mean that, Scott? Seriously, even though I might ignore you?'

'I'll be there, you'll see.'

'Yes, all right.' I smiled. 'It's usually around half nine.'

'Right. And we'll talk some more tomorrow.'

'Yes.'

'See you, Martha.'

'See you, Scott.'

19. Scott

Friday lunchtime we walked on the field. Kids're always in a good mood, Fridays. Nobody bothered us. I'd been thinking about Martha's sister.

'How old's Mary?' I asked.

'Twenty-one or twenty two, I think.'

'Was she at this school?'

'Yes.'

'Did she get the hassle you get?'

'I suppose so. I was only a baby so I don't really know.'

'How old was she when she left home?'

'Sixteen.'

'Why'd they kick her out?'

'Because . . . she was disobedient. Father couldn't control her.'

'Oh.'

Killer was in the cloakroom. He stopped me. 'Remembered any of those names yet, Scott?'

'No, sir.'

'Had any more trouble?'

'Not really, sir.'

'Good. Keep thinking, lad.'

'Yessir.'

At afternoon break I said to Martha, 'I think we should leave separately at hometime. Don't want Killer thinking we're going out together or something.'

'He might not be there.'

'No, but he might be. I'll go first, wait for you by the bus shelter.'

'OK.'

'So it's on for tomorrow?' I asked, when she joined me. Killer had been by the gate, so I was glad we hadn't walked past him like a couple. The shelter was full of rowdy kids whose weekend had just begun. We walked on a bit.

71

Martha pulled a face. 'Mother might not send me, Scott. She doesn't always.'

'No, but if she does?'

'If she does I'll see you. I don't know what we'll do though.'

'I told you. I'll walk you partway home, carry a bag.'

'Seems a lot of trouble for you, just for that.'

'It's no trouble. I like you. I want to see you.'

'I'm glad. I should go now.'

I looked at her. 'What d'you *do*, evenings? I mean, don't you ever get out?'

She shook her head. 'Both my parents work. Father has his round, Mother works the evening shift at the toy factory.'

'So you've got the house to yourself?'

'Yes.'

'So why can't you go out? Is it full of treasure or something?'

'I've got jobs to do.'

'Me too, Martha, but *all* the time?'

She nodded. 'All the time. I'm off now.'

'I could phone you. Or you me. That'd be OK, wouldn't it?'

'No, Scott, it wouldn't. I'm not allowed to use the phone, and anyway there's a lock on it.'

'Doesn't stop *incoming* calls.'

'No, but you mustn't. They'd know.'

'It's not fair.'

She sighed. 'No it's not, but it's the way things are. See you.'

The way things are. I didn't half wish I could change the way things are. For her, I mean. I fantasized about it, dawdling home. She was a prisoner in a dark castle. Rapunzel, maybe. I was a handsome knight. On a white horse, naturally. It was dark and wild, with lightning and thunder. Black, twisted trees thrashed their bare branches against the sky. I rode up to the castle. The drawbridge was up, the portcullis down. Light glimmered through window-slits. The Righteous lurked on the battlements with crossbows and boiling pitch but I fought my way in, threw her across my saddle and galloped away through a squall of arrows.

Not a lot of that going on in Scratchley in 1998.

20. Martha

It was a beautiful morning. Sun shining. Birds singing. I love April. I hummed one of Satan's latest tunes as I walked down Taylor Hill, swung left on Rickelrath Way and headed for Asda, swinging my plastic bag. Rickelrath is Scratchley's Twin Town in Germany.

My brain was nagging me and I couldn't quite drown it out with the humming. *Will he be there?* it nattered. *Will he be there? Will he be there?* 'I don't flipping know, do I?' I said aloud. 'You'll have to wait and see.' I tried telling myself it wouldn't matter if he wasn't but it doesn't work, lying to yourself.

Anyway, he was. I saw him straight away at

the car park entrance, leaning on the attendant's kiosk. He saw me at the same time and straightened up, grinning. 'They let you loose, then?'

'Yes.'

'Cleaning your cage out, I expect.'

'Cage?' My heart lurched. 'What d'you mean?'

'Hey!' He thumped me lightly on the arm. '*Joke*, Martha. Lighten up – it's spring.'

'Oh, yes. Sorry. I'm glad you came.'

He nodded. 'I'm glad *you* came. Let's get in before the crowd.'

We got a trolley and went up and down the aisles, him pushing, me crossing stuff off the list. I never knew shopping could be such fun. Scott swerved the trolley about, pretending to ram other shoppers, making screeching brake noises so that people turned to look at us. When I went to skip the sweets and biscuits aisle he yelled, 'Best bit coming up!', grabbed my arm and steered me and the trolley into it. 'I can't buy any of this stuff,' I protested. 'It's not on Mother's list.'

'Stuff Mother's list.' He plucked Mars and Rolos from the shelves and dropped them in the trolley. I shook my head. 'I've no money for sweets, Scott.'

'I have. I've got more dosh than Camelot, so come on.'

He swerved, screeching, into the next aisle, tossed a couple of Cokes in the basket and strode on. I followed, trying to keep up and read the list at the same time. If I missed something out, Mother would go mad. Scott was fifteen metres in front of me, grabbing bags of salt and vinegar crisps. I was horrified and happy. I started to giggle. He waited for me and we charged on together, me laughing so much I could hardly see for tears. My stupid brain kept nattering on about someone from church seeing us, but I wasn't listening. I think this was the most fun I'd ever had. At the checkout he shoved a ten-pound note in my hand. I gasped. 'Where'd you *get* this, Scott?'

'Made it myself,' he grinned. 'I'm a forger.'

'You're a madman.'

'That too.'

Outside he said, 'You don't have to go straight away, do you?'

I'd cooled down a bit. Mopped my eyes. I looked at him. 'I do, usually.'

'Yeah, but there aren't Cokes and crisps and choc bars to see to, usually.'

'What d'you mean, *see to*?'

'Scoff, of course. I didn't get 'em to look at.'

'We can't eat all this.'

''Course we can. Can't take it home, can you?'

'No, but you could.' I didn't want him to, though. I wanted to feast, just for once. Mother says feasting's for pagans, who can't control themselves.

Scott shook his head. 'I came a long way, Martha. Hung about. Splashed out on this stuff. You can't just walk off.' He smiled. 'I know a place where we can sit and scoff the lot. Say you'll come.'

I gazed at him. 'You know what you are, don't you?'

'Yeah, a madman. You told me.'

'You're a pagan.'

He rolled his eyes. 'A mad pagan forger. Maybe you better run before I get one of my funny turns.'

I shook my head. 'I think I'll take a chance, Scott. Just this once.'

21. Scott

I took her to the café in the park. I knew kids from school might be there and I didn't care. Anyway, as it happened there was just some old guy with a racing paper and a mug of tea. He'd tied his dog to a table-leg.

'Is he a Righteous?' I joked.

She was worried about being seen by someone who knew her folks. She chuckled. 'Oh, yes. You can always tell 'em by their dogs and dirty rain-coats.'

She was trying. She really was.

I got us Cokes. We had our own, but you can't sit at somebody's table and not buy anything. We unpacked our stuff and started in on the crisps. 'What will you tell your mum?' I asked.

'Oh, I'll say Asda was packed or a till went down or something. It always varies, the time I get back.'

'Great. We could do this every Saturday if you want.'

She shook her head. 'I told you – I don't always come. Sometimes Father shops Friday afternoon, sometimes Mother does it herself.'

'Well, what about us getting together other times, then? Evenings, maybe.'

'My parents work, remember? I don't get out.'

'I could come to you.'

'No.' She gazed at me. 'You must never do that, Scott. Promise.'

I chuckled. 'OK, I promise, but remember I'm a pagan, and a pagan's promise isn't worth much.'

'Don't joke. I really mean it. Don't come to the house. Ever.'

I sighed. 'OK, OK. Have some more crisps.' I shoved the bag across. 'And lighten up, Martha – this is supposed to be fun, remember?'

We were on to the Rolos when Gerry Latimer showed up. He was looking for someone and we weren't it, but he came across anyway. 'Hi. Seen anyone . . . Paul, Simon?'

I shook my head. 'No, just us.'

He looked at the stuff on the table. 'Someone's birthday?'

'No. Have a Rolo, unless you think it's contaminated.'

He struggled with his conscience for one point five seconds before grabbing a sweet. 'What you two doing here, then?'

'We just got married. At Asda. Two quid, and they throw in all this stuff.'

'Yeah?' His mouth fell open. Not the world's brightest guy, old Gerry.

'Oh, yes. You could drag Tracy Stamper down there but you better hurry – it's for two weeks only.'

He was taking it all in. I reckon he might have fallen for it if Martha hadn't cracked up laughing. He looked from her to me and from me to her, and a slow grin spread across his big dumb clock. 'You're winding me up, right?'

I nodded and stood up. 'Me and Martha have to go now, Gerry. Why don't you sit down and polish this lot off?'

He goggled. 'All this? D'you mean it, Scott?'

'Sure. Come on, Martha.'

I took the bags and we strolled back, over the footbridge and out on to Rickelrath Way. Martha puffed out her cheeks and blew. 'I'm totally pogged, Scott. I've never eaten so many goodies in my life.'

I grinned. 'Do you good. Something to remember tomorrow, in church.'

She giggled. 'The Righteous'd have a synchronized fit if they knew.'

Halfway up Taylor Hill she put a hand on my arm. 'Better not come any further. Someone might see.' She took the bags. 'I've really enjoyed myself this morning, Scott. Thanks for coming.'

'I enjoyed it too, Martha. See you Monday.'

'Roll on,' she murmured, starting uphill, and that was the best bit of all. You don't hear a lot of kids saying roll on Monday.

22. Martha

Sunday I was on edge till after morning church. If I'd been seen with Scott the day before, church is where Father would find out about it. When nothing was said on the way home or over the stew, I knew I could relax. Though it was the usual dreary Sabbath, it felt really different because of Scott. At last somebody actually liked me, enough to put himself out to be with me. It felt so good I wanted to tell someone. I wished more than ever I had Mary's address. She often mentions her friends, and I longed to tell her about mine. Still, it was no less real just because I had to keep it secret.

Monday felt different too. It's amazing, the

power of friendship. The kids jeered and shoved me around just the same as always, but somehow I didn't mind. They chanted at Scott too, at lunchtime, because he brought sandwiches and sat with me instead of having a proper meal. 'Your mum making *you* a pretend uniform is she, Snotty,' sneered Simon, 'so you'll match that bag-lady you hang out with?' We ignored them, and they didn't dare actually attack because Killer was on the lookout for bullies and everybody knew it.

I left the house that evening, as an experiment. I didn't *go* anywhere. I just walked about to see what would happen and nothing did. I was out an hour and a half and when I got back everything was the same. I thought, *If I can take an hour and a half, why not two hours, or two and a half?* I was thinking about Scott. Seeing him. Maybe going to his place. Not that night of course, but some other.

Possible snags. What if Father phoned home for some reason and got no reply? I'd never known him phone, but there's always a first time. Well – I could say I was in my room. You can't hear the phone from my room. And the same excuse would do if someone knocked on the door and got no answer. But suppose someone *did* knock, and Abomination was kicking up a fuss? There was nothing I could do about that, except check the creature was asleep before I left and hope if a caller heard anything he'd think it was a puppy or something.

OK – suppose Mother was taken ill at work and sent home? That happens, though it never has to Mother. That'd be the end of me for sure, but how likely is it?

Or what if one of the neighbours saw me go out and mentioned it later? Not much chance of that. None of the neighbours talk to my parents, who go out of their way to discourage neighbourliness.

What if the house caught fire? Well, if everybody thought about *that* before going out, nobody'd ever go anywhere, would they? People take chances all the time. They have to, so why not me?

Don't think I wasn't scared. When Mother came in I was sure she'd know I'd been out but she didn't seem to, and neither did Father half an hour later. I hugged myself, giggling, in the privacy of my room. When I was little, Father used to say that if I did something bad, even when he wasn't there he'd know, and I believed him. It was amazing the things he *did* find out about, but of course I realize now it had more to do with the thousand eyes of the Righteous than *his* all-seeing eye, or even God's. *They're just people*, I told myself. *They don't know everything.*

Lying in bed that night I asked myself why I hadn't tried my experiment far sooner. What had I been waiting for? I already knew the answer of course, deep down. The one-word answer.

Scott.

23. Martha

A card came Tuesday morning, from Mary. I was in the cellar when the post arrived, but when I came up for breakfast it was by Father's plate, torn in two. I pretended not to notice it, and when breakfast was over Mother picked it up and dropped it in the swingbin with the scraps.

I can never rescue a card in the morning, because I leave the house before my parents. What I do is, I wait till evening when I have the place to myself. By then, the card might have porridge on it, or fish-skin or gravy. It's a messy job retrieving it, though not nearly as revolting as cleaning up after Abomination.

This one was from Wolverhampton. It was a

picture of a church – St Wulfruna's – and it was addressed to me. This is what it said:

Dearest Marfa,

It seems ages since I wrote. No – I haven't moved again, poppet. Wolverhampton is close to Birmingham, so Annette and I come here some-times on Saturdays, for a change. Can I still call you poppet, by the way? You must be quite a big girl by now. I often wonder what's happening to you, and to a certain other person, though I'll never know about that. Are you happy, Marfa? It's not easy to be happy.

All my love,

Mary

It's not easy to be happy. Does that mean Mary's unhappy? I don't see how it can. She's free, and she's got Annette. Like I've got Scott. If this card had come last week I'd have said, *No, Mary, I'm not happy*, but now the answer is *yes, yes, yes.* I lie on my bed, sending this joyful answer to my sister. She must be picking up my signals, or why would a card come just as I'm wishing I could tell her about Scott? I concentrate, sending *I've got a friend*, *I've got a friend*, over and over.

I don't go out. When I finish transmitting I clean up Mary's card, mend it with sellotape and put it under the floor with the others. I've got thirty-two now. It'll be a bit sad if she keeps sending them after I've gone, won't it?

24. Scott

'Mum?'

'Yes, love?'

'You know that girl at school, Martha?'

'Ye-es.' She says it like I'm about to say we're getting married. It's Tuesday night. Dad's out. I've been dreading talking to Mum about Martha, but there's stuff I need to know and I can't wait any longer.

'Her dad beats her.'

Mum looks up from the *Radio Times*. 'Beats her? How do you know, Scott?'

'She told me. And she's not allowed out at night, and she daren't bring anyone home.'

'Hmm.' Mum pulls a face. 'I must say she

looked a bit like that when I saw her through the window last week.'

'Like what?'

'Oh, I don't know. Downcast, I suppose. Thin and pale, and those clothes . . .'

I nodded. 'They pick on her at school, Mum, because of her clothes. She belongs to this church – the Righteous. She has a rotten time.' I looked at her. 'It's against the law, isn't it, beating someone?'

Mum nodded. 'Yes, Scott, I believe it is.'

'So can't we *do* something, Mum? Tell someone? I feel really sorry for her.'

Mum nodded. 'I can tell you do, darling, but it's difficult . . . I mean, you can't go barging into other people's lives just because they're different from yours.' She sighed. 'You see, Martha may be exaggerating, Scott. Dramatizing herself. Girls do, sometimes. If her parents belong to a strict religious sect, her life *will* be different from most kids' lives and she may be unhappy about that, but this beating business isn't bound to be true. It could be a story she tells to get sympathy.'

'No.' I shook my head. 'No it's not, Mum, I can tell. I've seen her folks – we drove past them on Wentworth Road. They're seriously weird. They chucked her sister out of the house years ago, for practically nothing. Isn't there *anything* you and Dad could do?'

Mum looked at me. 'Those scratches you came home with the other day. It wasn't a game at all, was it? You got them defending Martha, didn't you?'

I nodded, staring at the carpet, feeling myself go red. How do parents *know* stuff like that? 'Yes.'

She sighed. 'Well it was very brave of you, Scott, and I'm glad you've befriended this poor girl, but I don't see how your dad and I can interfere. I mean – it might help if we could meet her. If you were to bring her home so we could talk to her. Get to know her a bit.'

I shook my head. 'I can't, Mum. I told you – she doesn't get out. And anyway she wouldn't talk. She's scared. Her dad doesn't like her talking to people.'

'How sad. Well.' Mum shrugged. 'You must go on being kind to her, Scott, and hope things sort themselves out.' She smiled. 'They usually do, you know, in the end.'

Thanks, Mum. Thanks a bunch.

25. Martha

The kids weren't bothering me as much now that Mr Kilroy was looking out for bullies, but there was one place he couldn't go and that's where they got me.

The girls' toilet, Wednesday afternoon. I was sitting in one of the cubicles, giving Scott time to walk past Killer without me when I heard whispering, then the sound of a tap running. Somebody counted softly: *one, two, three,* then *GO!* and water came flying over the door and under it at the same time. I couldn't dodge. One lot landed in my lap, the other drenched my socks and shoes. My gasp was followed by whoops of laughter and somebody started hammering on the door while several voices chanted, *Raggedy-Ann, Raggedy-Ann, wet her knickers in the can!* I leapt up and tried to dash the water off my skirt but it was no use. I was soaked. 'Come on out, Ma,' yelled Tracy Stamper, 'unless you want another shower.'

I had no choice. I slid back the catch and came out and they jeered and pointed and shoved me around. There were four of them. Stamper of course, and Thelma Rigsby and Gemma Horton and Felicity Wardle. *Raggedy-Ann, Raggedy-Ann, wet her knickers in the can!* A few stragglers had stopped and were looking at me, nudging one another and smirking. They hadn't been there when the water was thrown. They thought it was true, what Stamper and them were chanting. 'I didn't!' I cried. 'It was them. They did it.' I was nearly crying, but if anybody believed me they didn't show it. They booed and guffawed and turned away, drifting out into the yard. Soon, only the bullies were left.

'OK, Ma.' Stamper grabbed the collar of my blouse and slammed me against the wall. 'Say this after me. I'm a dirty little slut.'

I shook my head. 'No.'

She tightened her grip till I was nearly choking. 'Say it.'

'No.'

She turned her head. 'Fliss – more water.' Felicity Wardle filled a paper cup and brought it towards me, grinning. I struggled, but I couldn't get free. Felicity slotted the cup into Stamper's free hand and she stretched up and emptied it over my head. The water ran through my hair, down my face and into my blouse. Stamper let go my collar, stepped back and drove her fist as hard as she could into my stomach. It was like being hit by a truck. Everything went grey. I doubled up and fell to the floor where I lay like a comma, gasping and moaning. 'Come on,' growled Stamper and they walked away, leaving me to manage the best way I could.

When I finally got up I had to be sick into one of the basins. I rinsed it round and trailed outside. The yard was deserted but Scott was waiting by the shelter. He stared.

'What the heck's happened, Martha? You're wet through. Who . . . ?'

'Doesn't matter.' My stomach still hurt like anything. 'I've got to go. Listen.'

'What?'

'Meet me tonight, seven o'clock.'

'Where? I thought . . .'

'End of Dinsdale Rise. Can you make it?'

'Sure, but you look awful. I think I should walk you home.'

'No.' I pushed him away. 'I'll be all right. See you at seven.'

I don't know why I did it. Arrange to meet him I mean. Must've been a brainstorm. Or a message from Mary, carried on the wind. Be brave. Be brave. Be brave. Anyway I'd done it and that was that. I know it sounds like a lie, but I felt better straight away. The ache left my stomach, and by the time I'd walked up Taylor Hill my clothes were almost dry. I could hardly wait for dinner to be over and my parents to leave. Abomination seemed to be in a docile mood. I prayed it might continue.

26. Scott

I was there at ten to. I'd told my folks I was meeting someone, but didn't say who. We were halfway through April and it was light till quite late. They weren't worried.

She was five minutes early, and had on the same shapeless grey dress she'd worn to Asda. 'Hi,' she smiled. 'What d'you want to do?'

I hadn't really thought about it. Our meeting was her idea and I'd assumed she had something in mind. 'Why don't we just walk,' I suggested, 'and talk.'

'What about?'

'Well – you could start by telling me what happened at hometime.'

'Oh, that.' She pulled a face. 'Stamper and her mates chucked water over me in the bog and I got a punch in the stomach. I threw up, but I'm OK now.'

'That Stamper's a total veg.' I didn't know what else to say. I turned into Old Grange Lane which is long and narrow with trees that meet overhead, like walking through a dim green tunnel. Couples like to park there after dark, but we had it to ourselves now.

'I didn't know this was here,' she said. 'It's nice.'

I nodded. 'Yeah. Discovered it the day after we moved here. Leaves weren't out then.'

'Oh.'

'You . . . managed to get out, then?'

'What? Oh, yes.'

'Only you said you couldn't. Ever.'

'I know, and it was true. I'll get in awful trouble if Father finds out, but I'm trying to be brave, like Mary.' She smiled. 'Mary sent a message, you see. Be brave.'

'Didn't your folks see it?'

She chuckled. 'It wasn't that sort of message, Scott. It came through the air, from Mary's mind to mine.'

'Yeah, right.'

'No, I mean it. I've been sending to her since I was six. Now she's sending back.'

I shook my head. 'You're barmy, Martha, d'you know that?'

She shrugged with a dreamy smile. 'Maybe I am, maybe I'm not. Anyway I've decided to be more like my sister, if only to spite Father.' She laughed. 'Jezebel, he calls her.'

'Why?'

'After Jezebel in the Bible, of course.'

'Why – what did *she* do?'

Martha glanced at me. 'She was a fornicator, Scott. Surely you know the story?'

'No. Never heard of her.' I grinned. 'I know what a fornicator is though. They come here by the million at night, in cars.'

'How d'you know?'

'Seen 'em. Lovers' Lane, the locals call it. They'll start rolling up in an hour.'

'We better go, then.'

I nodded. 'Why don't I take you to my place, Martha? We could have a Coke and you'd meet my parents.'

She shook her head. 'I daren't. They'd think I was your girlfriend or something.'

'Would they heck. And what if they did? I don't care.'

'I do though. I'd *die*.'

'Rubbish. You'll like Mum, she's really nice, and I think Dad'll be out.' I smiled. 'Not that Dad's not nice too. I'm not saying that. So why don't we, Martha, eh? Say yes.' I really wanted her to agree, so Mum could start helping her.

We'd stopped. She stared out across a field that had cows in it. I waited. She was chewing her bottom lip. After a bit she nodded. 'All right,' she murmured, 'I'll come, but I mustn't stay long. I want to be home by eight and it's a fair way.'

'Magic!' We turned and began retracing our steps. Mostly I was glad, but I knew Mum and Dad would wind me up mercilessly afterwards for bringing a girl home. I tried not to think about it.

27. Martha

'Mum, this is Martha.'

'Oh . . . hello, Martha. You and Scott are on the same table at school, is that right?'

'Hello, Mrs Coxon. Yes, that's right. He sometimes lends me his ruler.' What a stupid thing to say, but I was really nervous.

Mrs Coxon chuckled. 'So the ruler brought the two of you together, eh?'

'Oh, we're not together, Mrs Coxon. Not like . . .' I felt my cheeks burn. Goodness knows what I'd have said if Scott hadn't interrupted.

'Where's Dad?' he said.

Mrs Coxon frowned. 'Martha and I are talking,

Scott. Your dad's gone over to Brian's to lo his new computer.'

'Sorry, Mum.'

He'd got me off the hook though. Mrs Coxon took my jacket and showed me where to sit. Scott sat beside me at the kitchen table, but not too close. His mother hung my jacket in the hallway, then brought Cokes from the fridge and a plate of Kit-Kats. As the two of us sipped and nibbled she bustled about the kitchen, lobbing questions to keep the conversation going.

'So, Martha, what do you like to do in your spare time? Are you a TV and computer freak like Scott?'

'No. We haven't got a TV or a computer, Mrs Coxon. I have jobs to do in the house, and I read quite a lot.'

'Hmm. I wish we could get Scott interested in books.' She smiled. 'Perhaps your influence will rub off on him, eh?'

'I don't know.' I was looking round her kitchen. It was gorgeous, like a kitchen in a magazine. I'm going to have one just like it someday. Light, bright and shiny. No cold tiles. No dark corners.

dear? *Point Horror*, *Sweet*
you into fanzines?' She was
washer. At our house, I'm the
ok my head.

d books like that, Mrs Coxon. Or
maga   got Arthur Ransome and Enid
Blyton and lot of school stories, and *Little
Women*. When I was younger I read *Alice in
Wonderland*. That was my favourite. And I read
the Bible.'

'Very good. I had *Alice* too, and *Little Women*,
but I liked the Nancy Drew stories best. Did you
ever come across her, Martha? Nancy Drew, girl
detective?'

'I don't think so.' I looked at Scott. 'They're not
in the school library, are they?'

He shrugged. 'Dunno. They sound like girl's
books. I read Pete Johnson's, when I read at all.'
He grinned. 'The Internet's my thing. Dead
educational, though Mum doesn't think so, do
you, Mum?'

His mother sighed. 'I can't see how talking to
some lad in Florida about favourite rock bands is
going to help with your GCSEs, Scott. There *is*
educational material on the Net, but I don't notice
you downloading it.'

'No, well, a guy's got to have fun sometime, Mum.' He chuckled. 'Curling up with Nancy Drew just wouldn't do it for me and anyway, was *she* the reason you got eight O-levels or whatever?'

'It's hard to say, dear, but going to sleep at half past nine after a chapter certainly made me brighter next day than if I'd sat up half the night surfing the Net.'

She was really nice, Scott's mum. Talked to us like equals, you know? Asked sensible questions and actually listened to our answers. Not like Mother, quoting the Bible every two minutes, showing no interest in anything that goes on outside the house or church. I could have sat there for ever but I left at twenty to eight. Mrs Coxon offered to run me home – she has her own car – but I didn't dare let her, and I didn't dare let Scott walk me either. I hurried away along Dinsdale Rise and it felt like leaving the real world behind and descending into the twilight zone.

Because that's what my parents' house is. Their house, and their life. The twilight zone.

28. Scott

So, Mum – what d'you think?' We'd watched Martha go out of sight before closing the door.

Mum smiled. 'I think she's a very nice girl, darling. Bit shy, but that's to be expected if she hardly goes out.'

'That's not what I meant. D'you think she's the sort to tell lies?'

Mum shook her head. 'I don't know, Scott. She was only here forty-five minutes, for goodness sake.'

'I know, but you must've got *some* idea. Can you see her lying to get sympathy?'

'No dear, I can't. As far as it's possible to

tell, I'd say she answered my questions with the plain, unvarnished truth.'

'So you'll help her?'

'Oh, Scott!' Mum treated me to her exasperated sigh. 'I don't know what you think I can do. Obviously Martha's unhappy at home and it's easy to see why. She's not allowed to do the sorts of things other children do. She doesn't have the possessions most children take for granted. Most children in our society, I mean. And the poor creature must stick out like a sore thumb at school, if her uniform's anything like that thing she had on this evening. Her parents must be deeply insensitive but you see, that's not a crime, and unless they're breaking the law there's nothing anybody can do.'

'Beating her's illegal.'

'I know, dear, but there's no proof. If your dad and I went to the police and told them the Dewhursts beat their daughter, the first thing they'd ask for was proof. When we said we had none, they'd refuse to act.'

'Well . . . would it be proof if *Martha* told them?'

'I doubt it. She'd have to show the marks or something.' Mum looked at me. 'You see, that's another thing. If she's beaten as she claims, I'm surprised someone at school hasn't noticed marks on her body. A PE mistress, perhaps.'

I shook my head. 'Doesn't make her a liar. Maybe her rotten dad's smart enough not to leave marks.'

Mum nodded. 'You may be right, dear, but the problem remains. Nobody can do anything without proof of wrongdoing, no matter how sorry they feel.'

I was mad. *Really* mad. Mum'd asked me to bring Martha home and I had, and now here she was saying she couldn't help anyway. I felt like going berserk. Smashing something, but I didn't. I just looked at her and said, 'I'll find a way to help her, Mum. Proof or no proof.' I wished I felt as cool as I sounded.

29. Martha

I was home by five past eight. Nearly two hours to spare. It was dusk and everything looked the same. No fire-engines. Nothing stuffed through the letter-box. No neighbour waiting to ask about the peculiar sounds coming from our cellar. I could probably have stayed longer at Scott's. I wished I had. I checked on Abomination, then continued my campaign of rebellion with an hour of Radio One. I danced to the music because I felt like it. Nothing – not even the fact that this house was a dungeon – could make me sad tonight. Just after nine I switched off, re-tuned the set and went up to my room. Nine's my bedtime. If either of my parents comes home and catches me downstairs, I'm in trouble.

Next morning Mr Wheelwright mentioned the Hanglands Expedition. It was a day I'd been dreading because there was no chance of Father letting me go. All the kids knew. I could feel them watching me as Wheelie told us the money had to be in by the first of May. Seventy pounds. 'Hands up those who are definitely going.' He did a quick count. 'Right. Hands up those who *think* they'll be going.' Another count. 'Uh-huh. Anybody definitely *not* going?' Slowly I raised my hand. It was the only one. Wheelie nodded and scribbled something on his pad. Tracy Stamper kicked my ankle. 'Never mind, Rags. You never know – your folks might win the Lottery.' The rest of the table sniggered, except Scott, who gave Stamper a dirty look and me a quick smile.

At break Scott said, 'I wish you were coming to Hanglands, Martha. It won't be the same without you.'

I shook my head. 'Nobody else thinks that, Scott. They're glad I'm not going.'

'They'd probably rather *I* didn't, come to that.' He pulled a face. 'I've a good mind to drop out.'

'No, don't. Not for me. It's nice of you, but I don't want you to.'

He shrugged. 'Well, we'll see.'

I smiled. 'It was great last night. Your mum's terrific.'

Scott frowned. 'She's OK I suppose.'

'OK?' I laughed. 'You're really lucky, Scott. Nice home, normal parents. I wish I lived at your house.'

'Huh! You'd soon see the other side of Mum and Dad if you did, Martha.' He grinned. 'Nothing to stop you coming tonight though. We could finish those Kit-Kats.'

I shook my head. 'Better not, two days on the trot. Your mum'll think I'm your girlfriend.'

Scott nodded. 'She does already, so you might as well come.'

'I daren't. Not tonight. I *will* come again soon though, I promise.'

'Well, how about me coming to your house?'

'*My* house?' I shook my head. 'It's impossible. I told you – I'm not allowed to bring *anyone* home, let alone a boy.'

'Who'd know, with your folks out working?'

'It's not just that, Scott. Our house is awful. Cold and dark, with no nice things in it. If you saw it you'd stop being my friend.'

'Would I heck! I don't care about your house, Martha. It's not yours anyway, it's theirs. I *want* to see where you live, so I can think of you there whenever I want to.'

'Well . . .' I sighed. 'I'll think about it, all right?'

He smiled. 'Fair enough. And in the meantime I'm going to have a word with Dad about Hanglands.'

I looked at him. '*What* about it?'

He winked. 'You'll have to wait and see.'

30. Scott

'Dad?'

'Uh-huh?'

'You know that girl at school – Martha?'

'Oh, yes.' Dad lowered his newspaper and gave me an amused look. 'Your mother told me you brought a girl home. Starting a bit young, aren't you? When I was twelve I was only interested in aeroplanes.'

I should've known he'd say something like that. I shook my head. 'She's not my girlfriend or anything, Dad. We're just friends, and I . . .'

'Oooh ah!' He looked across at Mum. 'Heard that one before, haven't we, love – just good friends?' Mum chuckled.

'Well, it's true.' They were getting to me, probably because I wasn't sure myself that Martha was just a friend. I certainly spent more time thinking about her than any friend I'd had before. I tried again. 'The thing is, she's the only kid in Year Eight who's not off to Hanglands and I don't think it's fair, just because her parents won't give her the money, and I was wondering if we . . . if you could pay for her, Dad.'

Dad's grin faded. He folded his paper, slid it on to the coffee table and looked at me. 'Son,' he said, 'that's not the way it works. People have reasons for the decisions they take, and they have their pride, too. This girl's parents might have a perfectly good reason for not wanting her to go to Hanglands.' He shrugged. 'Maybe they're frightened she'll have an accident, canoeing or abseiling or something. It might have nothing to do with the money and even if it has, imagine how they'd feel if some other kid's parents offered to pay. If they couldn't afford it they'd feel ashamed, and if they were just being stingy they'd feel angry.' He shook his head. 'There's an old saying, Scott. *Fools rush in where angels fear to tread*, and I'm afraid this is a case in point. It doesn't do to rush in, interfering in other people's lives. They won't like you for it, and you may end up doing more harm than good.'

I could have given him an argument. I could have said, *I thought we were supposed to help one another*, but I didn't. I know my dad. Once he's made his mind up, that's it. I was just glad I hadn't told Martha beforehand. That'd have been an even bigger bummer.

31. Martha

A favourite saying of Mother's is *Ask, and ye shall receive,* so I decided to try it out. I wouldn't have done it a few weeks ago but this was the new Martha. Martha, the sister of Mary and the special friend of Scott. Even so, I waited till Father had gone.

'Mother?'

'What is it, Martha?' She was getting ready for work.

'It's the Hanglands Expedition soon, and Mr Wheelwright wants the money in by the first of May.' I said it as though I fully expected to go.

She stopped in the middle of buttoning her cardigan. 'Why are you telling me about the

Hanglands Expedition when you know full well we can't allow you to go? Who do you think would look after the house, see to Abomination, while your father and I were at work?'

'It's only three days, Mother.'

'*Only* three?' She snorted. 'I suppose you wouldn't care to ask your father to take *only* three days off work so you can go, would you?'

'I thought . . . *you* might stay home, Mother. Just this once.'

'Oh you did, did you? You thought I might not mind losing twenty-four pounds in wages *and* forking out whatever ridiculous sum they'd want for teaching you how to paddle a canoe? It's going to be *really* useful to you in your adult life isn't it, knowing how to slide down a cliff? People will be queueing up to employ you.'

I shook my head. 'It doesn't matter, Mother. I didn't really expect to be allowed to go, even though you've often said to me, *Ask, and ye shall receive.* At least I know *that's* a nonstarter, don't I?'

She turned drip-white. Screamed at me. '*Don't you dare quote scripture at me, young woman. Wait till your father gets home – you'll receive what you've asked for then all right.*'

I didn't though. I didn't receive. Oh, he came stamping up the stairs, muttering. Working himself into a temper, but I'd shoved my chest of drawers across the door. You should've heard the language. Satan would've blushed. He stamped back down at ten past ten, growling about what he'd do to me in the morning, but when the time came he didn't do anything. I think Mother's sensed something about me. Some change. I bet she told him to lay off. Well, I *know* things don't I? Secrets. And I'm growing up. They can't pray that away, or beat it out of me either. *Time is on my side.* That's not in the Bible but it's true. I bet if I pushed hard enough I'd even get to Hanglands, but I'm not bothered.

Would *you* want to stand on the edge of a cliff with twenty-eight kids who hate you?

32. Scott

Friday we fixed up to meet outside Asda, same as last week. 'Remember I might not come,' she warned. I felt sure she'd be there, but at twenty to ten Saturday morning I recognized her mother stumping across the car park under the dead rat she wears instead of a hat.

It really peed me off, because it was drizzling and I'd been there half an hour. I'd planned on taking Martha to the library to check out the *Nickelodeon* studio. I could still go of course, but it wouldn't be the same.

I had a sudden daft idea, which was to follow Mrs Dewhurst round the supermarket. Don't ask me why. Maybe I thought I could learn something about Martha's home life by watching what the old bat chucked in her trolley, or perhaps I was just bored. Anyway I tailed her and grabbed a basket from the stack.

I read once that the music they play in these places sort of hypnotizes customers so they pick things up without meaning to. They're supposed to wander up and down the aisles in a trance and arrive at the checkout with a trolleyful of stuff they don't remember choosing. I don't know if it's true but if it is, it certainly didn't work on Martha's mum. She shot through the place like a dose of salts, missing out the interesting aisles and grabbing maybe one item each from the boring ones. I could hardly keep up with her and I wasn't buying. When she screeched to a halt at the checkout, her stuff only just covered the bottom of the trolley. Flour, sugar, lard, bag of spuds, washing powder, Pampers, oatmeal and soap. That was it. I'd dropped a bar of choc in my basket so I could queue behind her. Her coat was about four million years old and ponged of mothballs. To pay, she clawed coins out of a beat-up purse and counted them one by one into the girl's hand. She had very thin legs, with sticky-out veins like worms hibernating in her stockings. When I got outside she'd gone.

I didn't go to the library. We've got a modem and surfing's cheap at weekends, so I went home and wound up some woman in Florida. Told her I was a twenty-two-year-old brain surgeon with a Roller and a mansion in the country and she said *how fascinating*. Her name was Scarlett and her brain was OK, but she thought maybe I could help her in another way, because she was lonely. When I said I was really twelve she went off line without a goodbye. I sat gazing at the screen, wishing Martha was on the Internet.

Fat chance.

33. Martha

Sunday morning, Pastor Fenwick preached to the text *That every man should bear rule in his own house.* It's in the Book of Esther, and I don't believe it was coincidence made him choose it right after my little rebellion. I suspect Father'd had a word in his ear. Anyway I had to sit for three quarters of an hour between my parents while the Pastor slagged off kids who disobey their fathers. There were other kids in church, but it felt like every word was aimed directly at me. When we got home, Father carried his tool-box up to my room. I could hear him banging and scraping about up there as I helped Mother prepare the meal. I was scared. I thought he might be prising up floorboards looking for my books, my *Girl Talk* mags and – especially – Mary's postcards. I couldn't even imagine what he'd do to me if he found I'd been hoarding those for the last five years.

When he came down he put his tools away, rinsed his hands, blessed the food and started eating. I was pretty sure he hadn't found anything, but anyway I went up there as soon as I could. The floor was OK and at first I couldn't figure out what it was he'd done. Then I noticed the chest of drawers had been fixed to the wall with two L-shaped brackets. I checked and found he'd done the same to my wardrobe, my bedside unit and the bed itself. He keeps the key to my door lock, so there was now no way I could prevent his coming into my room. I didn't mention it, either then or later, and neither did he, but it made me more determined than ever to leave this miserable dump the minute I turned sixteen. That this was four years in the future depressed the hell out of me, but perhaps as time went on things would get easier.

Like they did for Esther.

34. Martha

An awful thing happened on Monday night. Mother had been gone about ten minutes and I was washing the dishes to the sound of Radio One when there was a knock at the door. I dried my hands on the tea-towel, switched off the radio and when I opened up Scott was on the step.

'Surprise!' There was a sheepish look behind his smile. I didn't smile back. I was shocked for one thing, and for another he didn't deserve a smile.

'I told you not to come here,' I hissed. 'How'd you know *I*'d answer and not Father?'

'I watched him drive off, Martha. Saw your mum leave too. I'm not daft.'

'You are, Scott. You are daft, or you wouldn't be here.' I glanced up and down the road. 'You better go before somebody sees you.'

'Nobody'd see me if I was inside, would they?'

I shook my head. 'I can't . . . I'm not allowed to ask anyone in.' I started to close the door. It was the last thing I wanted, to shut it in his face, but I was scared. It only needed someone from church to come by and that'd be that.

He stuck his foot out. The door bounced off his Nike. I didn't dare let him go on standing there. I stepped aside. 'Come on then, quick.' He came in. I closed the door, leaned my back against it and looked at him. 'OK, you're in. Now what?'

He shrugged. 'I dunno. I don't have to stay long. I just wanted to see you . . . you know, where you live.'

'Yes, well.' I gestured at the dim hallway. 'This is it. I told you it was horrible.'

'It's not horrible.' He looked at me. 'Do I get to see any more, or are we going to stay out here till it's time for me to go?'

'We can . . .' I nodded towards the kitchen. 'I was washing up. You can wipe if you want.'

He glanced around the kitchen and nodded.

'Nice. Sort of . . . old fashioned, you know – like a kitchen in a movie?'

'Sure.' I handed him the tea-towel. '*The Addams Family*.' He didn't contradict me, just looked embarrassed. I shoved my hands in the suds, wishing he hadn't come.

35. Scott

I wiped the last item and hung the tea-towel on the rail. Martha was drying her hands. I could tell she was mad at me and I was embarrassed. The house – the bit I'd seen so far – was really grotty. Not dirty. I don't mean that. I'm talking about dark paintwork, drab wallpaper and out-of-date fittings. There were no houseplants or flowers and yet there was an impression of clutter, of things chosen without care, crammed in corners and littering every surface. I knew that if I lived here I'd be seriously depressed *without* the bullying and the weird parents. No wonder she hadn't wanted me to come.

'D'you want to see my room?' Her tone was

leaden with resentment. I felt like saying *no, it's all right, I'll leave now*, but I didn't want her to think I couldn't wait to get out so I smiled and nodded.

It was up two flights of stairs, the second flight dark, narrow and creaky. It was the sort of place where women get bludgeoned to death with brass candlesticks in old black and white movies and you don't see the actual murder, just shadows on the wall. It smelled of damp.

'This is it.' I'm not kidding, the door squealed as she pushed it open. I saw a threadbare carpet and a grimy little window in the slope of the roof. The heavy furniture was fastened to the wall.

'Cosy,' I said. Well, what *can* you say?

'Yeah, right.' She indicated a wooden chair. 'Sit down if you like.' She sat on the bed and stared at the carpet.

There was an awkward silence, which I broke by saying, 'You don't have posters or anything, then?'

She shook her head. 'Not allowed, unless you count that.' I looked where she nodded. It was a framed text done in needlework. *Thou, Lord, seest me.*

'Did you sew it yourself?' I asked, for something to say.

'No, my gran did, when she was a little girl.'

'Oh.'

I didn't know how to keep the conversation going. Martha was ashamed of her home. I'd have felt the same if it were mine. I couldn't comfort her.

After a minute she brightened a bit and said, 'I know – I'll show you my secret stuff.'

I frowned. 'Secret stuff?'

'Ah-ha.' She got up and crossed to a corner of the room, where she knelt down and turned back the thin carpet. There was a loose floorboard. She lifted it, set it aside and started pulling stuff out of the hole. Four books. Some magazines. A rolled-up poster with a rubber band round it. A wad of postcards. She held up the postcards. 'From Mary. She's been everywhere. D'you want to look?'

I didn't. Not right then. I'd just remembered something from Saturday. Something odd. I shook my head. 'Not just now. Martha?'

'What?' She twisted round to look at me, still on her knees.

'Who were the Pampers for?'

She turned away and began putting things back in the hole. 'Pampers? I don't know what you mean.'

'Your mum bought Pampers at Asda.'

'Disposable nappies?' She was really busy, crouching over her hidey-hole. 'She can't have. And how would you know anyway?'

'I tailed her, stood right behind her at the checkout.'

She turned, the floorboard in her hands. 'Why, Scott? Are you spying on my family or something?'

I shrugged. 'Not spying, no. I was curious, that's all. And bored.'

'Weird thing to do, follow somebody round Asda. I hope she didn't notice you.'

'Why should she, Martha? Your mum doesn't know me from Adam.'

'It's just that if she thought . . . if she suspected I was seeing somebody at Asda, that'd be the end of my shopping expeditions.'

'Relax. As far as your mum's concerned I was just another customer.' I looked at her. 'You haven't answered my question.'

She shook her head, slotting the board in place. 'I don't know, Scott. She must've been getting them for somebody – a neighbour, perhaps.' She stood up, smoothing her skirt. 'I think you'd better go now. I'm scared in case Father finishes early.'

'OK.' I stood up and followed her out of the poky room and down the stairs. In the hallway she put a hand on my sleeve. 'Are we still friends, now that you've seen my place?'

''Course we are, you plank. I told you – I don't care about the house. See you at school, eh?'

She opened the door, glanced up and down the road. 'Yes. Take care, Scott. I'll see you tomorrow.' She watched from the step as I set off down the hill. I turned once to wave and she waved back, but when I turned a second time the door was closed.

36. Martha

Talk about a narrow squeak. He'd not been out of the house fifteen seconds when Abomination set up a howl. The cellar door's right there in the hallway. What the heck could I have said if he'd heard?

I had to see to the creature straight away or I think I'd have collapsed. It wasn't till I'd finished that the narrowness of my escape hit me and my legs went rubbery. I could hardly get up the cellar steps. I staggered into the front room, flopped in an armchair and sat shivering in spite of the evening sunlight streaming through the window.

'Course we are, you plank. Well, yes, but you

don't know what we've got in our cellar, do you Scott? I showed you *my* secret stuff, but not ours. Not the family secret.

When I was little I used to have nightmares about the monster in the cellar. I thought it was Mary. Don't laugh, Scott. Please don't laugh, because it isn't funny. There'd been noises in the night, see. Lights. Muffled footsteps. In the morning there was no Mary but we had this thing in the cellar, this Abomination nobody must know about. I thought Mary had changed in the night, that she'd somehow *become* this creature. Well, I was only six. And that's when the nightmares started. I'd wake screaming, but my room was at the top of the house so nobody heard. Nobody came.

Try to imagine, Scott. I thought people changed. That I might fall asleep a little girl and wake up as something they'd have to keep in the cellar. It had happened to my sister so why not me?

I realized eventually, of course. When the post-cards started coming. That's why I had to save the postcards. They drove away the nightmare. Kept it away. Mary was somewhere else but she was still Mary. She'd been in this town and that, so she couldn't be in the cellar. They saved me from going mad, those cards.

Trouble is, I've started to wonder lately whether the truth isn't every bit as ghastly as the nightmare.

37. Scott

I was in bed by nine but I couldn't sleep.
Thoughts chased one another round and round
the inside of my skull like bikers on a wall of
death. Pictures, too. Bits of Martha's house. Her
face when she saw me on the step. The awful
room she'd be in right now, thinking about me or
trying to transmit a message to her sister with
her mind. *Martha calling Mary. Come in, Mary. Are
you receiving me? Over.*

She's crazy about her sister, that's for sure.
Those dumb postcards. *She's been everywhere.
D'you want to look?* I should've said yes. Probably
hurt her feelings, saying not just now. I'll make a
point of asking to see them next time, if there is

a next time. 'Course there'll be a next time. Just 'cause she went in and shut the door before you'd finished waving doesn't mean . . .

That's how it was going. Round and round. No wonder I couldn't sleep. It was ten past eleven when I had the idea. Brilliant idea. Something I could try for Martha that she couldn't try herself.

The Internet. What if I managed to contact Mary on the Internet? A long shot, I admit, but better than telepathy. I got out of bed, switched on the computer and selected AOL. There's a site called TRAVEL that has a message-board. Martha says her sister travels, so maybe she checks out the message-board. Maybe. I typed in this message:

Martha Dewhurst would like to hear from her sister Mary, somewhere in England. Contact SCOXON *881@AOL.COM*

I'd just posted this when my door opened and Dad looked in. 'Do you know what time it is, young man?'

'Sure, Dad, it's on-screen. Eleven seventeen.'

'Exactly, and you have school tomorrow. Switch off now and get into bed.'

134

'OK, Dad.' I signed off and shut down, thankful that my message hadn't been on-screen when he stuck his head round the door. I suspect that, if he'd read it, he'd have accused me of rushing in where angels fear to tread.

38. Martha

There's one thing in my hidey-hole I didn't let him see. It's nothing much. Just a clipping from the newspaper with CHILD HELPLINE and a number. I keep it in case a day comes when I can't stand it any more. One evening, a few months ago, I thought that day had come so I called the number. I meant to let it all out, including Abomination, and have done with it once and for all. I'd no idea what would happen, but I felt sure that whatever it was couldn't possibly be worse than the way things are:

A woman answered. *Hello, caller. You're through to Child Helpline. My name's Doris and I want to help you. Won't you tell me what's the matter?*

She sounded sort of old and *really* kind, but when it came to it I couldn't do it. My voice wouldn't work. I stood with the phone to my ear and she said, *There's no need to be afraid, caller. You can say anything you want to, and nobody will ever know you called. Please talk to me so I can start to make it better.* I couldn't though. I hung up and collapsed in the chair, crying.

I know she's there though, Doris. There's a picture of her in my mind. Big and cuddly with strong arms and soft eyes, and I can call her anytime. *Count your blessings* is one of Mother's sayings and I do, lying in bed. One, Scott. Two, Mary. Three, Doris. Mother wouldn't see these as blessings of course but there's a saying: *One man's blessing is another man's abomination.* That's from the Book of Martha.

39. Scott

I was specially nice with her, Tuesday. Told her I'd enjoyed seeing her place. Even remembered to mention the postcards – said I'd love to see 'em next time. I didn't mention the Internet though. Well – it was such a long shot. I mean, not all that many people are on the Net, and the chances of Mary being one of them seemed pretty slim. Also I felt uneasy, like I'd butted in on a family conversation or something. She was nice back, but said we better not fix to meet up. Not tonight. I didn't argue, but I thought maybe I'd just show up on her step again and I did, and that's how I found out the truth.

The truth. Yes. You remember I said if you get

to really know a weird person you'll find there's a reason why they're the way they are? Well, listen up and tell me if I was right.

I got to her place around seven fifteen. I was standing on the step thinking, I hope she's not going to be mad at me, when I heard this noise, this sort of howling. It was muffled, like it might be coming from a distant part of the house and my first thought was, it's her. They're beating her. That's why she wouldn't fix to meet me – she knew her folks weren't working tonight and they're not. They're in there belting the daylights out of my girl. I actually *called* her that inside my head – my girl – and before I knew what I was doing I was hammering on the door with both fists. What the heck I'd have done if old man Dewhurst had opened it I don't know because I wasn't feeling like a knight in shining armour. I was scared spitless if you must know, but anyway it didn't happen. Nobody came. When I stopped pounding everything was quiet for a second then the howling started again, except howling's not quite right. It wasn't howling. Not exactly. It was a mixture of hoots and screeches, and between these a sort of bubbling drone that made my skin crawl.

I wanted to leave but I couldn't. Not without trying one more time. I waited for a break in the noise then knocked again, this time more urgently. All this did was to start whatever was in there screeching again. I turned and hurried along the path feeling sick. I was halfway down Taylor Hill when I saw Martha coming up.

40. Martha

When I spotted him coming down towards me I was glad and mad at the same time. Glad to see him, mad because he'd obviously been up to my place. Glad and mad had a quick wrestling match inside my head and glad won. I decided I'd be nice to him.

As soon as I saw the expression on his face I knew something was wrong, and I'd a fair idea what it was. No chance of a happy half hour now, and no point acting mad either. *Ye shall know the truth*, I thought, *and the truth shall make you free*. John, chapter eight, verse thirty-two; another of Mother's favourites. She wouldn't be all that thrilled at my revealing this particular bit of the truth but blast it, I'd had enough. It was time to talk to someone.

He didn't mess around either. 'What the heck you *got* in that house of yours – a vampire?' Dead tactful. I shook my head and he said, 'What, then?'

'Abomination. I expect you heard Abomination, Scott. Somebody was bound to, eventually. His voice is getting stronger, you see.'

He looked at me. 'Abomination? What *is* that – some sort of name? Is it a dog, or what?'

I shook my head. 'No Scott, it isn't a dog. Look – if I tell you, you mustn't tell anyone else, not even your mum. D'you promise?'

'I . . . I dunno.' He shook his head. 'Depends what it is, Martha. I can't promise to keep quiet about something when I don't know what it's going to be, can I?'

I didn't answer straight away. A struggle was going on inside me because this wasn't really about me. It was *their* secret, not mine. Can you give something away that's not yours? Scott put his hand on my arm. 'Listen,' he murmured, 'if it's something private – something that's nobody else's business, I won't tell.'

I nodded. 'It's private all right. A family thing, only . . .'

'What?'

'Only I'm not sure it ought to be, Scott. I've thought loads of times about telling someone: a teacher or a woman called Doris or even the police, only I couldn't stand it if Mother and Father got into trouble. They think it's the right thing, you see. They wouldn't do it otherwise. They'll have prayed about it. Listened for the still, small voice. Oh I know they're weird, Scott, but they're good people. Good people. They do what they think's best. What they believe God wants.' I broke off, shaking my head.

He squeezed my arm. 'Share it, Martha. Tell me, then we can both decide. It might be easier, two thinking about it instead of one.'

I looked down, biting my lip. It was so hard after all this time to let the words out. If Scott and I had been on the phone I think I'd have hung up. I stared at the pavement. Cars swished by. After a while I took a deep breath and murmured, 'Abomination's a boy, Scott. A little boy. He lives in the cellar, in a cage.' I looked up, my tears making a blur of his shocked face. 'I'm his auntie,' I choked.

41. Scott

I didn't say anything, just stood there waiting for it to sink in. Martha was crying into a tissue I handed her. People were passing but nobody took any notice. If you don't look, you don't have to get involved. After a bit she looked up and said, 'Say something, like what you think. I don't care.'

I shook my head. 'I don't know what to say, Martha. It's too much. A shock.' I think she sort of laughed but she was blowing her nose at the same time so it was hard to tell.

'A shock. Yes. You won't want to be my friend now, I bet.'

'Yes, course I will, but that's not what matters, is it?'

'What *does* matter, Scott? I need somebody to tell me because I'm sick of keeping it to myself. What am I supposed to *do*?'

I pulled a face. 'God, Martha, don't ask me. It needs someone older. An adult. We have to talk to somebody.'

'Not the police!' Her voice was suddenly shrill. 'You promised, Scott. Father and Mother mustn't get in trouble, I told you that.'

'I *know*, but . . .'

'You promised.'

'No, I *didn't*, Martha. Only if it was nobody else's business.'

'Well it isn't anyone else's business. It's family. *My* family. I shouldn't have told you.'

'Yes, you should. I mean, you were right to tell, only I don't know how to help. This kid – who's his mum?'

She laughed. No doubt this time. 'Who d'you think, if I'm his auntie?'

'Mary? He's *Mary's*?'

'Yes, of course, you plank.'

'But you said . . . I thought Mary was – you know – *nice*.'

'She *is*. She's terrific. She's the best sister in the world.'

145

'And she lets her kid live in a *cage*? I wouldn't call that being nice, Martha. I'd call that . . .'

'SHE DOESN'T KNOW!' *That* got people looking, I can tell you. Her shout. I never knew Martha had a shout like that.

'Ssssh!' I hissed. 'Everybody's staring.'

'I don't care.' She looked furious. 'How could you think Mary'd let somebody live in a cage? Her own kid? She thinks they had it adopted when it was a few days old. They told her they would but they didn't, because of the Righteous.'

'The Righteous?' I stared at her. 'You've lost me, Martha. What have the Righteous got to do with it?'

She sighed, shook her head. 'You don't understand, Scott. You'd have to be a member to understand. We can't just . . . babies are for *married* people, see, and Mary wasn't married, and if my parents had . . . look, we can't stand here talking about this.' She looked at her watch. 'Come home with me and I'll try to explain, but you mustn't do anything.' She gazed at me. 'You mustn't *do* anything, Scott, like – like try to take the kid or something. D'you promise?'

'Well . . . yeah.' I nodded. What the heck would I do with a kid anyway? Nothing was further from my mind. We set off up the hill.

42. Martha

I told him, sitting on the bed in my room. Got out the postcards. Showed him Mary's references to the kid in the ones she wrote to Mother and Father – those oblique references I hadn't understood for the first three years or so. I left him reading through the cards while I went down to see to Abomination. When I got back he'd finished and was staring at the floor. 'Well?' I asked, with one eye on the time. All I needed now was for one of my parents to walk in and find him.

He shook his head. 'I don't know how you've kept quiet all this time, Martha. It's an awful thing your folks have done. Awful. Normal people just don't do stuff like that.' His voice was unsteady, his face dead white. 'It explains the Pampers though. Can't have nappies out on the line, can you? Dead giveaway that'd be.'

I gazed at him. 'I didn't realize, Scott. You don't, when you're little. You think everybody's home's like yours. You assume other kids' parents are like your own. I was eight when I realized other mothers *buy* their children's clothes, they don't sew them. Before that I didn't understand why kids laughed at me. And I was nine before I worked out the truth about Mary. First I thought Abomination *was* Mary – that she'd changed in some horrible way overnight. Then for a long time I believed he must be my little brother, though I couldn't work out why he had to be a secret. I suppose I was ten when it dawned on me he was Mary's. I'd discovered you don't *have* to be married to start a baby, you see. It all fell into place after that, but by then I was used to the situation. I mean it didn't feel right, but it didn't seem strange, as it must to you. I wasn't shocked into action. It's always seemed important to me to protect my parents. Guard their secret . . .'

'Yes, but what about the *kid*?' He stood up.

'Living like a chicken in a cage with a name like Abomination. Still in nappies at six. We can't . . . just leave it, Martha. We *can't*. We've got to tell somebody. Listen.' He grabbed both my arms. 'What about Mary? What d'you think she'd do if she knew?'

I shook my head. 'I don't know, Scott, but she isn't going to know because I don't have her address.'

'What if I knew of a way to contact her? Would you let me?'

'I . . . I suppose so, as long as my parents didn't find out, but how could you possibly . . . ?'

'The Internet.'

'What?'

'The Internet. You know what that is, don't you? You've heard kids at school talking about it.'

'Yes, sort of, but you need special stuff, don't you? On your computer. The ones at school haven't got a . . . whatsit.'

'Modem. No, but mine at home has. I could post a message, hope she sees it.'

'But she'd have to have a . . . a modem too, wouldn't she? I can't imagine – brought up here,

like me. We don't even have TV. I can't see Mary
with a modem.'

'It needn't be Mary herself, Martha. Someone
she knows would do. Someone who knows her.
They'd pass on a message, I'm sure. Shall we give
it a whirl?'

'I dunno, Scott. It's such a big thing. I can't
think. Not now. Look, it's coming up to nine.
You'd better go. I'll have a think and let you know
in the morning. Is that all right?'

'Yes, I suppose. I mean, the kid's lived like that
all his life, one more night won't make much
difference. But we'll have to do something,
Martha, and pretty quick too.'

It was five to nine before I got him out of the
house. When he'd gone I ran upstairs and threw
up, I was so tense. I went to bed so I needn't see
my parents, but I didn't sleep. I was sending
messages all night. *Your baby's here, Mary, waiting
for you. Such a long wait. Come in, Mary. Over . . .*

43. Martha

'Where did you go yesterday evening, Martha?' Father, at the breakfast table. What a jolt. Somebody must have seen me so there'd be no use denying it. 'Old Grange Lane, Father. It's green and quiet.' I was praying I'd been spotted alone and not with Scott.

'Green and quiet.' I was amazed by the softness of his tone. A year ago he'd have been round the table with the rod in his hand. As it was, he remained in his place and there was no sign of any cane. Mother was ladling porridge into three bowls. She didn't speak, or even look at me. I nodded. 'I had to get outside, Father. A walk. Sometimes this house . . . does my head in.' It wasn't an expression I'd normally use. His eyebrows went up. 'Well, I'm sorry the home your mother and I work hard to provide is not to your liking, Martha. We do the best that we can, with the Lord's help. Did you by any chance . . . *meet* somebody in Old Grange Lane?'

'No, Father.' It wasn't a lie. Not quite. I'd bumped into Scott on Taylor Hill.

'So this house doesn't *do your head in* to where you can't help discussing family business with outsiders. That's good.' He leant forward, hands clasped on the table. 'Nevertheless you will not repeat last night's excursion or leave the house for *any* reason while your mother and I are absent. Is that clear?'

'Yes, Father.'

'Good.' He sat back as Mother placed a steaming bowl in front of him. 'Abomination seems more than ordinarily restless lately and needs constant attention.'

'Perhaps he needs his mother.' God knows what made me say it. I shouldn't have, because it was probably that which made Mother drop the bowl she was carrying. It smashed on the tiles, spattering globs of porridge all over the kitchen.

Father froze, the spoon halfway to his lips. 'He

has no mother, Martha. She died a long time ago.'

I forced myself to meet his gaze. 'No, Father, she did not. Her name is Mary, she's my sister and she sends postcards. And if she knew we'd kept her baby in our cellar for six years I don't know what she'd do.'

44. Scott

'Is anything the matter, Scott?' Mum over corn-flakes, looking concerned. Dad was gazing at me too.

I shook my head. 'No, why?'

'You were making funny noises in the night, dear. Shouting things. It was obviously a night-mare so I came and woke you. Don't you remember?'

'No.'

She chuckled. 'You spoke to me, but you must still have been asleep.'

'What did I say?'

'You won't believe me if I tell you.'

'Tell me.'

'All right. You sat up, gave me a really earnest look and said, *It explains the Pampers though, doesn't it?*'

'Did I?'

'You certainly did. Goodness knows what you were dreaming about.'

'Did I say anything else?'

'Not another word. I said, *Yes, dear, I suppose it does*, and you sank back into your pillow, fast asleep.'

'Huh.' I gazed into my bowl. 'Funny things, dreams. I don't remember anything about it.' I did though. A dark place. Somebody looking for me. Hunting me. A kid, horribly deformed, in a cage. Couldn't tell Mum about that though, could I?

She looked at me. 'It's just that sometimes nightmares are brought on by worry, Scott. Your dad and I have noticed you looking a bit pre-occupied lately, and we wondered . . .'

'Nothing's wrong, Mum. Honestly, I'm fine.'

'What about school?' asked Dad. 'Any problems there, son?'

'No.'

'Coping with the work, are you? Making friends? No bullying or anything like that?'

'No. I told you, I'm fine.'

'Because you know you can talk to us anytime, don't you? About anything? We're on your side no matter what. Remember that.'

'I will, Dad. Thanks.'

If only.

45. Martha

They kept me off school. I wouldn't have minded except it was the first of May. It was the deadline for Hanglands money, and Stamper and Linfoot and silly Pritchard would think I was wagging off because of that. I didn't try to explain this to Father because I knew it would make no difference. The truth is, he was scared, and so was Mother. I could see it in their eyes. They were terrified I might tell their secret. It's a good job they didn't know I'd already shared it with Scott.

That was the other bad bit. Scott. I was supposed to be telling him today whether to try reaching Mary on the Internet. I'd thought it over and over in bed and decided yes, and now I couldn't let him know. I wondered whether he'd go ahead anyway, and prayed he wouldn't tell one of the teachers instead.

I had to show where the postcards were, and of course they found my other stuff too. Father lost his temper and slapped my face. Mother said something to him on the stairs and he came back. I was curled up on the bed, crying. He sat down and started dabbing my tears with his hanky, murmuring that he was sorry. I felt like saying, *Bring my stuff back if you're sorry*, but I didn't. I didn't say anything. After a while he shoved the hanky in my fist and went away. I could tell by the slow way he walked that he knew the game was up. What he didn't know was that I'd give anything if the child could be helped without him and Mother being hurt. That I loved them, and that's what made it hard.

46. Scott

When Martha didn't turn up at school I was worried. What if her folks knew she'd let me into the house, told their secret? *Maybe she's a prisoner in that poky attic? Beatings? Bread and water?*

The kids made it heavy for me too. 'I notice Raggedy-Ann's wagged off,' whispered Simon as Wheely was collecting the last of the Hanglands dosh. 'Couldn't face the shame, I expect.' He pretended he was talking to Tracy but he was watching my face. I kept it blank, fishing stuff out of my bag.

Stamper nodded. 'I bet if you could sew fivers her mum'd have made her some.' The whole table laughed except me.

'Right,' spluttered Linfoot. 'They'd be twice as thick as real ones, with loose threads and crooked edges.'

'And *nearly* the right colour, but not quite,' added Thelma Rigsby.

Oh, they thought it was a great joke. Really funny. I ignored them.

I hoped she'd show up at lunchtime but she didn't. I'd brought sandwiches so we could talk and I ended up eating next to Felicity Wardle who said, 'Girlfriend wagged off, eh, Snotty?'

'Shut your gob, zit-features.' Not like me, that. I don't call people names, but I'd had enough and besides, I needed to think.

I couldn't get that kid out of my head. A kid in a cage. *Still* in a cage when a word from me would free him. *Fools rush in*, Dad says. In other words, mind your own business, but a kid in a cage – shouldn't that be *everybody's* business?

I thought maybe I'd bump into her on my way home, but I didn't. *She's locked up*, I told myself. *If she was free she'd have found a way to see me.*

Straight after tea I went upstairs and switched on my computer. I'd convinced myself Martha would have said yes, and anyway I'd no choice. People who'll keep a baby in a cellar for six years might do anything, and Martha was at their mercy. I'd already posted a message on the TRAVEL message-board, but there'd been no response. I decided the cyber cafés offered a better chance. Mary's last card had been posted in Birmingham and there was a cyber café – the Café Surf – in that city. Maybe someone who knew Mary was a regular there. Maybe.

I wrote a new message:

> *Will anyone who knows Mary Dewhurst, born in Scratchley but last heard of in Birmingham England, please ask her to e-mail* SCOXON *881 @* AOL.COM *for urgent news about a certain six-year-old child*

I hoped she was using her real name. I thought I'd better not put *her child* in case she didn't want her friends to know she had a child. *Six-year-old* would do the trick – she'd know which child I was on about, *if* she ever got the message.

Big if.

47. Martha

'You know, Martha, we couldn't get in touch with that . . . with Mary, even if we wanted to.' Thursday morning, doing the breakfast things. Her washing, me wiping. Father had slipped out to call at the office. 'She's never let us have her address, as any decent daughter would.'

'Can you wonder, Mother?' I clattered tea-spoons into the drawer. 'You called her Jezebel, made her leave her baby, drove her out. This is the first time you've spoken her real name, and the kid doesn't even *have* one – Abomination's not a name.'

'He'll get a name when he's baptized, Martha.

We haven't been able to arrange that up to now because . . .'

'Because you daren't let the Righteous know he exists.' I folded and hung the tea-towel. 'What about the truth, Mother? *The truth shall set you free*, but the three of us have been lying for years and years.'

She tipped the washing-up water down the sink and wiped the drainer with the dishcloth. 'You don't understand, Martha. They'd have driven Mary out anyway. The Righteous, I mean.'

'Would they? That's not very Christian. I thought we were supposed to love one another.'

'Love the sinner, hate the sin. That's our way.'

'Oh, you mean we show our love for sinners by turning our back on them?'

'They have to *repent*, Martha. Express regret. Jesus said *go, and sin no more*. Your sister showed no regret, only defiance. She made it pretty plain she'd no intention of mending her ways. Refused even to name the child's father.'

'She might have had a good reason, Mother.'

'Rubbish!' She peeled off rubber gloves, stacked them behind the taps. 'Your sister is no good, Martha. No good. You tell somebody about that child, and all that'll happen is they'll come and cart him off to some orphanage or other, and you'll have to go too because your father and I will be in prison. Is that what you want?'

I shook my head. 'Of course not.'

'Then keep quiet, child. It's not lying, it's keeping ourselves to ourselves. Your father and I have prayed about this, and the Lord has showed us how the child might soon be baptized and live a normal life.'

'Normal?' I looked at her. 'You mean like you? Like me? Is that what you think of as normal, because I don't. I've been bullied, Mother. Laughed at all my life because of the way we live. These stupid clothes. If *that's* all he's got to look forward to he might as well stay in the cellar.'

'Martha.' She held out her arms towards me but it was too late.

I shook my head, turned away. 'I'm off, Mother. Off to school. I don't want anything bad to happen to Father or you but something's got to be done and it will be.' I stumbled, half-blind with tears, out into the bright May morning.

48. Martha

The buzzer went just as I came through the gate, so there wasn't time to speak to Scott.

'Where were you yesterday, Martha?' goes Wheelwright.

'Sir, my mother needed me at home.'

'Have you brought a note?'

'No, sir.'

'Tomorrow, Martha, without fail. All right?'

'Sir.'

Stamper leaned across. 'Mummy send you out collecting rags, did she, for your summer outfit?'

'You're ugly, Tracy Stamper,' I hissed. 'Your posh uniform can't hide that.' I was amazed to hear the words coming out of my mouth. I don't know how I dared. The others were startled too, including Scott. His mouth fell open, then he gave me a look that made my heart soar.

'That's *you* told, Stamper,' he chuckled, 'and she's right. You've a face like a bulldog chewing broken glass.'

You should have seen her. Talk about furious. 'You wait, Rags,' she spat. 'You just wait till break.'

She didn't do anything at break. Never came near, and we weren't standing outside the staffroom window. Couldn't get the gang to join her, maybe.

'Scott,' I said, 'we've got to find Mary. I want you to use the Internet.'

'I already have. I'm trying the cyber cafés, and if that fails I'll post a spam.'

'Spam?'

'Yeah. Means posting the same message to loads of different newsgroups. You're not supposed to do it but this is an emergency. I also wondered if the Beeb might put out one of those S.O.S. messages. You know . . . *Will Charlie Farnsbarns, last heard of five million years ago in Outer Mongolia, please go to the Tracy Stamper hospital for the terminally ugly, where his mother . . .'*

167

'No.' I shook my head. 'Not the radio, Scott. My parents listen. Other Righteous. It'd get back. Better stick to the Internet – Righteous don't surf.'

He grinned. 'Just walk on water, eh?'

He wanted us to meet around seven. I shook my head. 'I can't. Somebody saw me, Tuesday night. Split on me to Father.'

'What happened? Did he . . . ?'

'No. He's stopped beating me, Scott. He's scared I'll tell somebody about the kid, but all the same I'd rather stay home evenings till we've got this sorted.'

'OK. I'll check the Net. What d'you want me to say if Mary gets in touch?'

'Tell her it's Martha, only spell it Marfa . . . M-A-R-F-A. It's her pet name for me, so she'll know it's genuine. Say her kid's in a cage in our cellar, and to come rescue him any weekday evening after seven or we get the police.'

He nodded. 'OK. We'll talk some more at lunchtime. And hey?'

'What?'

'It was terrific, the way you came back at Stamper. I really enjoyed it.' He grinned. 'Marfa.'

168

49. Scott

When someone's e-mailed you, Joanna Lumley's voice says *you've got post*. It didn't happen that Thursday teatime so I switched off and went out for a think. It was a warm, sunny evening and there were about a thousand people in Old Grange Lane so I went to the park and walked beside the river. There were plenty of people there too but I sort of screened them out. I felt like my head might burst with all the stuff going round and round inside it.

Mostly it was Martha. I think I loved her. I mean, it was obvious I liked her a lot, but surely you don't think about somebody every minute of the day and night just because you like them. I'd left good friends in Birmingham and, yes, I thought about them sometimes, but not like this. This was getting to be kind of an obsession. I'll tell you what I mean. I was by myself right now, walking along the riverbank thinking, and all the time I was talking to Martha. I don't mean aloud. I wasn't walking along talking to someone invisible like crazies sometimes do, but I was *imagining* her there beside me and we were having this silent conversation. I was talking to her in a way I'd never dare do if she were really there. *Martha, I've fallen in love with you. I know you're going to say we're only twelve, but it's true. I just think about you all the time. I want to look after you.* Stuff like that. It made me groan to think what Mum and Dad would say if they knew the state I was in. Life wouldn't be worth living.

Then there was the kid. Six years old and still in Pampers. What did he look like? He *sounded* like a wild animal the night I heard him through the door. What did Martha have to do when she looked after him? What, exactly? I've got a vivid imagination and I made myself feel sick thinking about it.

Why had I got involved anyway? If I'd joined everybody else in chasing Martha instead of making her my friend, I wouldn't know anything about her. Or Mary. Or the kid in a cage. I'd be off somewhere with my mates, enjoying myself, not traipsing along the riverbank like a loony, talking to someone who wasn't there. *Fools rush in*, Dad said. I was beginning to think he was right.

There was one bright spot. Tomorrow was Friday, and next Monday was the May Bank Holiday. Three days without school. I might see her Saturday at Asda, and Monday she might be able to . . .

There I go again. Oh, heck.

50. Martha

Any weekday evening after seven. God. We were talking about a kid's *life*, and it sounded like one of those notices you see when someone's selling a house. I thought it'd save hassle if our parents weren't there when she came, that's all.

Talking of selling houses, there was a shock waiting for me when I got home. I walked in the kitchen and there was Mother shoving stuff in cardboard boxes. Knives. Ornaments. Pots and pans. Boxes all over the floor. I said, 'What . . . ?'

'Moving.' She slid a full box aside and stooped for an empty one. 'Thanks to you.'

'What d'you mean, moving?' I could hear Father crashing about upstairs. 'How can we?

What about . . . ?' I nodded towards the cellar.

'We'll manage.' She was stuffing oven-gloves and tea-towels in the box. 'We'll have to, and it's all your fault. You and that . . . what's his name . . . Scott.'

'Scott? Why Scott? He hasn't . . .'

'You've been getting far too close to him, Martha. Your father tried to warn you but you wouldn't listen. We're different. Chosen. It doesn't do for us to mix with those who don't understand our ways. They make trouble for us. We have to go, now, before it's too late.'

'N . . . now?' Dread gripped me. 'You mean today? We're off *today*? What about school? Father's work? Where will we *live*?'

She swung the box on to a stack, grabbed another. 'It's a pity you didn't ask yourself all these questions a few weeks ago, child. Father's transferred to his company's Wharton branch and found a house to rent, so we'll live in Wharton. As for school . . .'

'But Wharton's miles away. Fifty miles at least. I can't be fifty miles away from . . . away from . . .'

'That boy?' She scoffed. 'Don't be ridiculous, Martha. You're twelve years old. A little girl. When I was your age I played with dolls and crayons, not boys. You'll forget him in a week, and quite right.'

I shook my head. 'No, I won't. He's the only friend I've ever had because of you. Because of the Righteous. I won't forget him because I won't go and you can't make me. If you try, I'll tell about the kid. I'll tell Mr Cadbury, the police, everyone. I'll tell Pastor Fenwick. You'll be cast out of the congregation as sinners and you'll both go to jail and I'll be GLAD.' My voice had risen and I screamed the word *glad*. Mother started towards me. I spun round to make a dash for the door and cried out. In the doorway, with a face like thunder crouched Father, his arms spread wide to catch me.

51. Martha

He locked me in my room. I kicked and wriggled all the way upstairs. 'You can't keep me locked up,' I gasped. 'Who'll look after the kid when you and Mother are at work?'

It turned out we weren't leaving till Tuesday. Something about the Bank Holiday weekend, but Father was owed some leave. He wouldn't work again till he started at Wharton.

'School,' I tried. 'You already kept me off Wednesday. If I don't show up tomorrow, they'll wonder what's happening.

'No, Martha, they won't.' He shoved me into the room. 'I spoke to Mr Cadbury on the phone. Told him I was being transferred at short notice.

You've left Southcott Middle, young woman.'

So that was that. He turned the key in the lock and went downstairs. I sat on the bed, dazed by the speed of events. Twenty-five minutes ago I'd said goodnight to Scott believing we'd meet first thing tomorrow. He was going to check the Net. Might have news in the morning, but now I wouldn't be there. I'd never see him again.

Oh, I didn't give up just like that. I tried to think of a way out. I'd heard of people picking locks and I searched for something to use. Something made of wire. I found a coathanger in my wardrobe, opened it out, made a little kink in one end and shoved it in the keyhole, but no matter how I jiggled and twisted it nothing happened.

I considered the window. It's a skylight – a grubby little thing in the slope of the roof but it opens. I stood on the chair, opened it and peered out. All I could see was a patch of sky, slippery tiles falling steeply away to the gutter, and the roofs of houses across the street. I'd pictured myself climbing out and reaching the ground by way of a fallpipe, but as soon as I saw that slope I knew I wouldn't go out there even if the house was on fire.

I fantasized briefly about scrawling messages

and throwing them out. *Help. I'm locked in attic. Kid caged in cellar. Tell police.* I'd have to use pages from my Bible or tear off bits of wallpaper because they'd taken my postcards and magazines. I actually ripped a flyleaf out of the Bible, but then realized I'd nothing to write with.

My one hope now was that Scott would succeed in finding Mary through the Internet before we vanished next Tuesday. It was a slender hope. So slender that I curled up on the bed and cried myself to sleep.

52. Scott

Friday morning I kept telling myself, *There's a million reasons people take a day off school. Sore throat. Sick in the night. Slept in.* But at break Thelma Rigsby and Tracy Stamper came charging across the yard to tell me Mrs Fawthrop was clearing Martha's locker.

'She's expelled,' gasped Rigsby, 'for scruffiness.'

'Lying cow,' growled Stamper. 'She's been sent to a special school for disturbed kids. I heard Chocky tell Wheely.' You could see they were both really pleased.

I hurried to the office. After a minute Mrs Fawthrop appeared with a bulging bin-liner under her arm. She's the school secretary. 'Yes, Scott, what can I do for you?'

'Miss, it's about Martha Dewhurst. I was wondering . . .'

'*What* were you wondering, Scott?'

'Miss, some of the girls are saying she's left. Tracy Stamper says she's gone to a special school.'

'Tracy Stamper is talking out of the back of her head as usual, but Martha won't be coming back after the Bank Holiday. That much is true. Her father's work is taking him elsewhere and the family is leaving Scratchley.'

'Where, miss? Where are they going?'

Mrs Fawthrop dumped the bin-liner on a chair and sighed. 'I don't think that's any concern of yours, Scott Coxon. If the Dewhursts had wanted you to know where they were going, they'd have told you. *I* can't.'

'But, miss, it's *really* important. Martha and me . . .' Should I tell? About the kid and everything? How would he ever be rescued if they vanished with him?

'Martha and you?' She twinkled like grown-ups do when they think they've discovered some kid's romantic secret. 'Don't you think you're a bit young for that sort of thing, Scott? Both of you, I mean. Anyway.' She smiled. 'She knows where you are, doesn't she. I expect she'll write if she wants to keep in touch.'

And that was it. Subject closed. Interview over. I felt so mad I decided there was no point trying to explain to her. She probably wouldn't believe me anyway. I turned and walked away, and when I got outside Rigsby and Stamper were parading round the yard holding hands, singing:

Raggedy-Ann, Raggedy-Ann
Ran away with Desperate Dan

Dan's not the only one who's desperate, I thought.

53. Martha

They let me out Friday. They had to. The kid was playing up like never before – screeching and yelping and throwing himself at the bars. I reckon he knew something unusual was happening. They left me to cope with him while they got stuff ready for the move. I tried to divert him with talk and toys and grub but he wouldn't settle. Everything I tried him with he chucked at me, and he kept trying to clamber out of the play-pen. In the end Father came and screwed down his night-roof and we left him to it. Turned Classic FM to full volume and let him scream.

After that I had to empty my drawers and wardrobe and pack all my clothes in a big old suitcase. They didn't lock my door, and when I'd finished I went down and helped Mother make a meal in the bare-looking kitchen. I was being really good, but it was just an act. What I wanted was a chance to slip outside if only for a minute, so I could leave a message for Scott.

I'd thought up this plan last night in bed. It was a desperate plan because it depended on three things. One, Scott had to have learned that I wasn't coming to school any more. Two, he had to come up Taylor Hill to try to find out more. And three, I had to put a message somewhere he'd see it before he came up our path. I'd written the message in big letters with a red felt-tip on a sheet of wallpaper Mother had lined my drawers with. It said: *SCOTT. DON'T KNOCK. PARENTS IN. WE LEAVE TUES. IF NO MARY BY MON, TELL YOUR FOLKS, TEACHERS, ETC. BUT WAIT TILL MON. LOVE, M.* It was folded in my skirt pocket, which also held four drawing pins. All I needed was a couple of minutes outside.

It was agony waiting, especially after half-three. Suppose Scott came up straight from school? He wouldn't knock because he'd assume my parents were home. Most likely he'd walk past a few times looking sidelong at the house, trying to see if anything was happening. Hoping to spot me through a window, maybe. He'd go away eventually and come back after seven, *and this time he'd knock*. I didn't dare imagine what would happen after that. I had to pin up that message somehow. I *had* to.

My chance came at half six. Mother had gone to work her last shift. Father, who'd been watching me like a hawk all day, had to slip upstairs to answer a call of nature. He must have thought the front door was locked or that I'd abandoned thoughts of escape, but he was wrong. The instant he was out of sight I was through that door and down the path, pulling the crumpled notice from my pocket. The blast from the radio masked any sound I might have made, but I knew I only had a minute. I ran a few metres downhill and pinned my notice to next door's fence, praying some busybody wouldn't rip it down and that it wouldn't rain. If it rained, my words would dissolve to a meaningless blur in seconds. I pushed home the fourth pin, turned and raced back to the house. By the time Father reappeared I was back in the kitchen, wiping the few dishes we'd left unpacked. I'd done my best. Now I could only wait.

54. Scott

What I wanted to do was shoot straight up to
Martha's after school. I nearly did, but then I
realized there'd be no point. If they'd left already
there'd just be an empty house, and if they hadn't
her folks would be there. I told myself they
couldn't have left today or Martha would've
known about it yesterday. More likely they'd go
over the weekend. I decided to go home, check
my e-mail, grab a bite to eat and get up there
around seven.

Oh, I didn't feel as cool as that sounds. No way.
And it wasn't just worry about the kid. I mean I
was worried, obviously – a day or two at the most
and there'd be nothing useful I could tell Mary if

she *did* get in touch – but mostly right then it was Martha. Me and Martha. Yes OK, I'm admitting it. I was crazy about her. In love, as Mum would probably say. *Scott's in love.* Big joke. It was no joke though. You'll know if it's ever happened to you. It tore at me all the way home. *She's going away and I don't know where. If I get to see her tonight she'll tell me where, but what if it's fifty miles away. A hundred. Two hundred. We'll never meet again. Never. Will she write? Does she feel the same as I do or will she forget as soon as she's in her new school, find some other guy?* I was nearly crying if you must know.

I went straight upstairs when I got in. Switched on, hooked up to AOL and selected e-mail. *You've got post*, goes Joanna Lumley. I swallowed, trying not to get excited. I've got five buddies who mail me. It was probably one of them. Only it wasn't. It was Mary, e-mail address ABAXT 779@ AOL.COM. The message read:

I'm Mary Dewhurst. What about the child? Is this a joke? If so you're sick, sick, sick. If not write ASAP, above address.

I sat gobsmacked, staring at the screen while precious time ticked by. I couldn't believe it. Such a long shot. The sender mentioned a joke. What if *this* was a joke? A flame? No way of knowing. I thought for a minute then wrote:

Mary this is Marfa. Come quick. M&F move to unknown location maybe today. Child has lived six years in cellar, answers to Abomination. Thanks for card of lady in fountain. Hope Annette well. Love Marfa.

That ought to do it. My misspelling of Martha's name, plus references to Annette and the post-card would tell Mary the message had to be genuine. I just hoped ABAXT would check her e-mail tonight and pass it on straight away. I suspected the address was Annette's, so I was hopeful. In fact I couldn't wait to tell Martha. I bolted my meal and shot out the door like a scalded lop. Mum and Dad must've thought I was barmy. Or in love.

55. Scott

Number one, Mary's message. She'll be so surprised. So *chuffed*, but we mustn't forget number two, the new address. I can e-mail that to ABAXT tonight in case the mad Dewhursts flit before Mary can get here. And when that's sorted there's number three. The big one. I'll have to ask her straight out, won't I, 'cause I won't get another chance. *D'you love me?*

Oh come *on* Scotty – get real. There's no way you're gonna say that. Not face to face. No chance. What if she laughed? She doesn't laugh much, old Marfa, but I bet she'd laugh at that. All right then, what about, *will you write? Postcards will do, like Mary, only more often if you can manage it. That's not too much to ask is it, after all I've done for you?*

No, I mustn't say that. Wouldn't be fair. She's got to *want* to keep in touch. So, leave out the last bit and say *will you write, 'cause I'll write to you?* Yeah, that sounds OK. I can manage that face to face.

This was the conversation I was having with myself as I trogged up Taylor Hill, and it turned out to be all for nothing because just before Martha's place I saw this notice pinned to a fence. At first I thought it was one of those signs sad creeps put up when it's someone's birthday. You know – HARRY SPACK IS FORTY TODAY – but it wasn't. It was for me. I couldn't believe it.

SCOTT. DON'T KNOCK. PARENTS IN. WE LEAVE TUES. IF NO MARY BY MON, TELL YOUR FOLKS, TEACHERS, ETC. BUT *WAIT* TILL MON. LOVE, M.

The word *wait* was bigger than the rest, but it was the word *love* that made my heart kick me in the ribs. *Love, M.* I stood gawping at this like a div instead of taking in the message. It was only when a Harley came roaring over the hill that I remembered what I was supposed to be doing

188

and realized I couldn't do it now. I got my brain in gear and tried to think.

Parents in, so I can't tell Martha that Mary knows the situation and might show up anytime. Not unless I knock and tell whoever answers the door. They'd flit straight away then, and they wouldn't leave a forwarding address.

The police? No. *Wait till Mon*. That's clear enough, isn't it? Trouble is, the situation's changed since Martha left this notice. *If no Mary*. But there *is* and she's coming, and Martha needs to know this without her folks finding out. How, though? *How*?

One thing I could do was get rid of the notice before her mum or dad saw it. I tore it off the fence, folded it roughly and shoved it in my pocket. Luckily there were no nosy pedestrians about, just the odd car whooshing by. I crossed the road and walked past the house on the other side. Everything looked the same. Martha wasn't at any of the windows. How the heck could I get word to her, tell her her sister was coming? Get her new address, ask her to write?

Suppose I hang around till Mary comes? There's bound to be ructions, and maybe I'll get a word with Martha in all the chaos. Slip her a note. Yeah, but she might not come till midnight, or tomorrow or even Sunday. Depends when ABAXT checks her e-mail. Can't hang around till then, can I? Dad'll have the police out.

There must be a way. Must be. I needed to think so why not do it here, in the shadow under this sycamore where I could keep an eye on the house? I could compose a note on a scrap torn from Martha's notice, just in case. I leaned on the wall, pulled a biro out of my inside pocket and began with my favourite word. Martha.

56. Martha

Nine o'clock. Starting to get dark and no sign of Scott. One half of me was relieved – the half that said he'd *wanted* to see me but had spotted my message. The other half kept whispering that maybe he hadn't come because he wasn't all that bothered. That half was desperate.

Mother was due anytime now, and I was dead scared she'd see my message. She shouldn't – the bus would drop her off at the top of the hill and she'd turn into our gateway without even glancing at next door's fence, especially in the dusk. But what if she did? What if the whiteness of the paper drew her eye and she got curious?

The phone rang. Father picked it up. I couldn't

191

see him because I was in the kitchen and the phone's in the hallway. He hung up straight away so it must've been a wrong number. I went on fixing supper. It rang again. Again I heard Father pick it up. A couple of seconds and it went down with a bang. Father came along the hallway muttering, and just as he reached the kitchen it rang for a third time. He went back, picked it up and shouted, 'WHO IS THIS? WHAT D'YOU WANT? I'LL HAVE YOU *TRACED* IF YOU BOTHER ME AGAIN.' *Slam* went the handset.

My heart was battering my ribs like the kid in his cage. Could it be Scott calling? Would he be that crazy? I swallowed, struggling to keep a hold on myself. When Father came in I said, 'Who was that, Father?' I hoped my voice sounded normal.

'Never you mind,' he growled. 'Your mother will be here soon.' Meaning *get on with it*. I lifted the kettle off the gas and poured boiling water into the teapot. My hand was shaking.

Mother came in carrying a bouquet which she flung on the worktop. 'Can you believe it?' she snorted. '*Flowers*, for someone who's moving in three days. What do they think I'm going to *do* – pack them and take them with me?' I bet she'd been a ray of sunshine at that factory, my mother.

It's a miracle they gave her *anything*. She obviously hadn't seen my message though.

'No brains,' grunted Father. 'Any of them. Like the idiot who phoned just now.'

'What idiot?' asked Mother, peeling off her cardigan.

'Oh, some young yobbo with nothing better to do. Three times, he called. Three times. Bothering decent folk.'

'What did he say?'

'Nothing that made sense. *Contact established. Mother ship approaching*. Science fiction freak by the sound of it. Soon stopped when I threatened to have him traced, I can tell you. No brains and even less guts, that's his type.'

I managed to act normal, I think, but I couldn't eat much. As soon as Father had given thanks I excused myself and went to my room. *Contact established. Mother ship approaching*. It was Scott. *Had* to be. The calls were his way of letting me know he'd found Mary through the Internet and she was coming. So not science fiction, Father dear. Science *fact*.

Beam me up, Scotty.

57. Scott

Old Dewhurst, yelling down the phone like that. Very near shattered my eardrums. Only way I could think of to alert Martha, those three calls. I was pretty proud of it, to be honest. *Contact established. Mother ship approaching.* Not bad thinking for a stressed-out guy in a callbox at nine o'clock at night. Of course it might not work, I knew that. If he didn't tell anybody, I'd have wasted my breath. That's why I rang three times, so he'd remember the exact words and be mad enough to repeat them in Martha's hearing. I didn't doubt she'd know what they meant – she's a sharp cookie, old Martha. So. I'd done all I could to tell her to expect Mary, but I hadn't found out where her folks were taking her or if she'd write to me. It was nearly dark when I left the phonebox and I knew I had to go home. I wondered if she'd show up at Asda in the morning. It wasn't likely, but I knew I'd be waiting there anyway.

I spent a long night picturing what might be happening up there on Taylor Hill. Mary descending on the family home like an avenging angel, battering good old Mum, throttling dear old Dad, snatching her kid and roaring away in a shiny red Porsche. Or maybe she'd do it a quieter way. Creep up the garden path, pick the lock with a credit card, tiptoe down the cellar steps. The Dewhursts wake in the morning to find the kid gone and no trace of how. I suppose I got *some* sleep but I didn't feel as though I had.

I was outside Asda before nine, and of course she didn't come. Of *course* she didn't. Probably Mary showed up last night five minutes after I abandoned my vigil. She could've brought the police. Anything could be happening up there this morning. *Anything*. I paced the carpark till half nine, then set off to see for myself.

58. Martha

I had a rotten night. Well, rotten in one way, thrilling in another. I got into bed without undressing because I expected Mary any minute, but the longer I lay there the more doubtful I felt about those calls. I mean, I'd no *proof* it was Scott. Father might be right – it could have been some sci-fi freak on alcopop. As time crawled by and nothing happened, this seemed more and more likely. And if it wasn't Scott – if Scott hadn't even been near – my notice would be on next door's fence in the morning for all to see. For Father to see.

I prayed. Not my usual bedtime prayer. This was the prayer of a screwed-up kid who's had just about enough. *Dear God, I know Mother and*

Father will have spoken to you about this, but it surely can't be right to keep a child in a cage. Maybe you told them and they misheard. I don't want to get them in trouble and I don't mean to be wicked. I just think a kid's entitled to some love and sunshine, and how did that get into my head if you didn't put it there? Please let Mary come soon. Amen.

I think I slept after that, because the next thing I knew it was light and I could hear a blackbird. I got up and straightened my clothes a bit, though my stuff always looks slept in anyway. I washed my hands and face, brushed my hair and went downstairs. My parents were at table. We said good morning. Mother served the porridge. The kid was kicking up a fuss below. It was just like any other Saturday morning. I wondered whether Scott would try Asda as usual.

'Mother?'

'What is it, Martha?'

'Do you need anything from the supermarket this morning?'

'I don't think so, thank you. We can make do till we move, and shop in Wharton on Tuesday evening.'

'Oh.' My heart sank. I'd hoped to remove my notice *and* see Scott.

'There's something you *can* do,' said Father. 'When you've attended to Abomination, you can take a screwdriver to your room and free your furniture from the walls, ready for the removal men.'

'Yes, Father.' If prayers are answered, Mary'd have come and none of this dreary stuff would be happening. *Prayers aren't answered,* I thought, as I trailed down those cellar steps for the two thousandth time. I was nearly crying.

A few minutes later I was wiping slop from round the kid's mouth when someone knocked on the front door. *Postman,* I told myself, guarding against the cruelty of false hope. I dropped the cloth in the basin and reached for the pack of disposable nappies. I heard Father turn the key, draw the bolt. *Some boring package,* I thought. *Tracts. A double glazing catalogue.*

'YOU!' Father's voice, startled and outraged at the same time. *Who? Scott? No.* A woman's voice. *Not . . . surely not Mary?* I rose to my feet, staring towards the steps. The kid, cold in his sodden nappy, began to grizzle.

'I want my child,' shrilled the voice. 'Give him to me NOW!'

'Child?' spluttered Father. 'Have you gone

MAD? The child isn't here. It was adopted, six years ago. We don't even know . . .'

'He's *there*, in that cellar. Martha e-mailed. Let me pass, or I'll . . .'

'E-mail? *Martha* e-mail? Now I *know* you're mad. There's no e-mail here. Lizzy!' He called to Mother. 'Come here and tell this lunatic . . . this strumpet, that her bast . . .'

And that's when something weird happened inside my head. Really really weird. I think it was the words *my child* that did it. I looked at the kid and it was like I saw him for the very first time *as a kid*. He wasn't the monster I'd once believed him to be, and he wasn't the nuisance I'd been saddled with. He was neither a chore nor a shameful secret; he was a child: a frail, beautiful, grey-eyed child who should be out in the sunshine with other six-year-olds, not cooped up and mucked out and fed through the bars like a battery hen. I gazed at him and knew at last the enormity of the wrong I'd helped commit.

I ran sobbing to the foot of the stairs. 'MARY!' My voice broke up. 'HE'S HERE.' Father growled an oath and there were sounds of a scuffle. Mother began to wail. I turned, scooped the kid out of the playpen and started up the steps. He was light. Almost weightless. Father was standing at the top with his back to me and his arms spread, blocking my progress and my sister's view but the end was in sight and nothing was going to stop me finishing it now. *Nothing*. I twisted sideways and rammed my shoulder into the small of his back. He didn't move much, but the woman got a glimpse of her child and that was enough. She flung Mother from her, side-stepped Father, snatched the kid out of my arms and half-ran towards the open door. The child covered his eyes with his hands and began to scream. It was the light streaming through the doorway. The sunlight. He'd never encountered such brightness. It seared him, and to find himself bouncing towards it in the arms of a total stranger must have been more terrifying than any of us can imagine. I was imagining what my parents would do to me after Mary had gone, when she paused and turned, her free hand held out towards me.

'Come on, Marfa, quick!'

The thought that I'd be rescued too hadn't entered my head but I didn't hesitate, following this thin, dowdy stranger out the door and down the path to where another stranger sat in the driving seat of an ancient car whose engine was idling. The last thing I saw as acceleration slammed me back in the seat was Mother on the doorstep looking like someone beholding the end of the world.

59. Scott

I was halfway up the hill when this beat-up Mini came down, trailing smoke. It was the clapped-out noise that made me look, and for a split-second my eyes locked with Martha's. I thought, *They're off. They're taking her away and I don't know where.* I meant, her folks. It wasn't till the car had passed and I was staring after it that I realized it wasn't theirs, and that the three people I'd glimpsed were all women.

That was Saturday. It's Monday now and I'm sitting on a bench in the park thinking about Martha, trying to cheer myself up counting the good things.

One, the kid's not in a cage, he's with his mother.

Two, Martha's not in that awful house. She's with the sister whose sad torn cards she hoarded all those years.

Three, it all seems to have happened without anybody learning the Dewhursts' secret so they're not in trouble, which is how Martha wanted it.

Four, she's away from Pritchard and Stamper and all those other donkeys at school.

Which leaves me. I can't pretend I'm happy, because Martha's gone and I love her. Oh, I know what Mum'd say. You *can't* be in love, Scott. You don't even know what it means. Well, she might be right in a way. Maybe I don't love Martha the way Mum loves Dad or I love Mum, but I love her just as *much*. There's different *sorts* of love that's all, and the more sorts the better if you ask me because you can't have too much love.

Are you thinking about me, Martha?

60. Martha, Mary, Jim, Annette

Thin, dowdy stranger. That's Mary all right. Nothing like the swashbuckling adventuress I've pictured all this time. Turns out she's been just as miserable as me. Moving on from town to town, working long hours at deadly jobs for bad pay, always looking for something without knowing what.

She knows now, or so she says. It was Jim. Jim, who used to be called Abomination. Annette reckons Mary's a different person now she's got Jim. He's absolutely gorgeous, but he's hard work. He can only do baby things so he's not at school yet, but all sorts of people are helping him. Mary's teaching him to talk. She reads him about ten stories a day and chats to him by the hour, and he's starting to chat back. What kills me is the way he lets me cuddle him as though I never was his gaoler, but that's how little kids do love, isn't it? Unconditionally. He even cuddles me back, which is far more than I deserve.

I've started at a new school but it's dead easy 'cause I wear bought clothes like everybody else. I don't get Raggedy-Ann any more. Some of the kids call me Ma, but in a friendly way. There's not much money so I'm not going on the school trip here either, but I'm not the only one and anyway I don't care.

I miss Mother and Father. I know that sounds like a lie but it's not. They did a wicked thing but they thought it was right, and now they've lost everybody. They've never tried to make me go back and I wouldn't go if they did. I expect they know I'm all right with Mary, that the pair of us will sin our way through this world and spend eternity together, somewhere a bit warmer. I sent them a card with my love and no address but I expect it's in the bin, torn in two.

I'm looking forward to Wednesday. It's Annette's half day off and she's promised she'll show me how to surf the Net. You know – the Internet.

Guess who I'm going to e-mail first.

THE END

ABOUT THE AUTHOR

Robert Swindells left school at fifteen and worked as a copyholder on a local newspaper. At seventeen he joined the RAF for three years, two of which he served in Germany. He then worked as a clerk, an engineer and a printer before training and working as a teacher. He is now a full-time writer and lives on the Yorkshire moors.

He has written many books for young readers, including many for Random House Children's Books. *Room 13* won the 1990 Children's Book Award and *Timesnatch* won the Junior Category of the 1995 Earthworm Award. *Abomination* was shortlisted for the Whitbread Award and won the Sheffield Children's Book Award. His books for older readers include *Stone Cold*, which won the 1994 Carnegie Medal, as well as the award-winning *Brother in the Land*. As well as writing, Robert Swindells enjoys keeping fit, travelling and reading.

NIGHTMARE STAIRS
by Robert Swindells

*I'm falling - falling down steep, narrow stairs - if
I hit the bottom asleep, I know I'll never wake.*

Every night Kirsty wakes up screaming. Every night
she has the same terrible nightmare - of falling
downstairs. But does she fall? Or is she pushed?

Then Kirsty discovers that her grandma died falling
downstairs and she begins to wonder: is the dream
hinting at a dark secret in her family? She has to
know the truth. But tracking a murderer is a
dangerous game, and as she delves into the past,
Kirsty uncovers a secret more terrible than
anything she can imagine.

A terrifying read from one of today's
master storytellers.

WINNER OF THE SHEFFIELD CHILDREN'S BOOK AWARD
FOR BEST SHORTER NOVEL

'Cleverly put together - funny as well as gripping'
Sunday Times

ISBN: 978 0 552 55590 6